'Welcome to The Larches, Eleanor. It's good to have you on board.'

Ellie felt relief wash over her as she reached for his hand. She had completely misread the situation, it appeared. Daniel wasn't thinking of rescinding his offer after all. His hand closed around hers and a frisson ran through her when she felt the strength of his fingers envelop hers. For some reason she couldn't explain, it felt right to have him hold her hand—right and wonderfully reassuring. Even though she knew nothing about him, she felt safe with him. Safe and cherished.

'It's good to be here,' she murmured, quickly withdrawing her hand.

She dredged up a smile, needing to rid her head of such nonsense. Daniel Saunders was her employer: no more and no less than that. He wasn't going to have any impact on her life outside of work…

Dear Reader,

When I had the idea for this book I didn't realise how much I was going to enjoy writing it—or that it would lead to a whole trilogy set in The Larches GP practice in the Yorkshire Dales!

As soon as Ellie and Daniel appeared on the page they had me hooked. Then, as I built the story around their budding romance, other characters started to clamour to have their stories told as well. It was a real snowball effect, and I hope you get as much pleasure from reading the series as I am having writing it.

Both Ellie and Daniel have a lot of baggage when they meet, and they certainly aren't looking for love. However, they soon discover that it isn't always possible to do the sensible thing. Whilst they both know it isn't the right time for them to have a relationship, they simply can't help themselves—even though they're sure it can't last.

Helping them realise that they can find a way around their problems was totally engaging. I agonised over the decisions they made, felt for them when they thought they had to part, and rejoiced when they realised they simply couldn't live without each other. Some characters are simply meant to be together. Like Ellie and Daniel!

Love,

Jennifer

THE BOSS
WHO STOLE
HER HEART

BY
JENNIFER TAYLOR

MILLS & BOON

First published in Great Britain 2017
By Mills & Boon, an imprint of HarperCollins*Publishers*
1 London Bridge Street, London, SE1 9GF

Large Print edition 2017

© 2017 Jennifer Taylor

ISBN: 978-0-263-06729-3

Our policy is to use papers that are natural, renewable and recyclable products and made from wood grown in sustainable forests. The logging and manufacturing processes conform to the legal environmental regulations of the country of origin.

Printed and bound in Great Britain
by CPI Antony Rowe, Chippenham, Wiltshire

Jennifer Taylor has written for several different Mills & Boon series, but it wasn't until she 'discovered' Medical Romances that she found her true niche. Jennifer loves the blend of modern romance and exciting medical drama. Widowed, she divides her time between homes in Lancashire and the Lake District. Her hobbies include reading, walking, travelling and spending time with her two gorgeous grandchildren.

Books by Jennifer Taylor

Mills & Boon Medical Romance

Saving His Little Miracle
One More Night with Her Desert Prince…
Best Friend to Perfect Bride
Miracle Under the Mistletoe
The Greek Doctor's Secret Son
Reawakened by the Surgeon's Touch

Visit the Author Profile page
at millsandboon.co.uk for more titles.

For Leo and the team at Cancer Care,
a huge thank you. You really are the best!

**Praise for
Jennifer Taylor**

'A superbly written tale of hope, redemption
and forgiveness, *The Son that Changed His
Life* is a first-class contemporary romance that
plumbs deep into the heart of the human spirit
and touches the soul.'

—*CataRomance*

CHAPTER ONE

SHE COULD HAVE been beautiful with that fine clear skin and those huge grey eyes. However, the severely cropped black hair and strictly functional clothing did nothing to enhance her appearance. As he took stock of the woman seated in front of his desk, Daniel Saunders found himself wondering why Eleanor Munroe had failed to make the most of her considerable assets. Was she *deliberately* trying to disguise her femininity for some reason, playing down the fact that she was a highly attractive woman?

'Right then, Dr Munroe, we may as well get straight down to business.'

Daniel dismissed that strangely unsettling thought as he picked up her CV. He skimmed through it once more, although he already knew the facts by heart. Dr Eleanor Munroe was thirty-five years old, with a birthday coming up the following month. She had read medicine at Cambridge and graduated with a First Class Honours degree. After completing her rotations at St Linus's Hospital in London, she had opted to go into general practice and had trained at a busy practice in Kent and subsequently been hired by them too. She had supplied references from the head of the practice and had added a codicil to the bottom of her CV that gave Daniel permission to phone and speak to her referee directly.

Although it was unusual to do that so early in the proceedings, Daniel had taken up the offer and he had to admit that he'd been impressed by what he had heard. According to her former employer, Dr Munroe was above reproach and any practice who hired her would be extremely fortunate to secure her services. It appeared that Eleanor Munroe ticked all the boxes on paper, at least, but he still needed to be sure that they could work together.

'A most impressive CV, Dr Munroe,' he said, glancing up. 'Backed up by the conversation I had with your former colleague. He was highly complimentary and even mentioned that you were in the running for a senior partnership. It makes me wonder why you decided to leave your last post when you were so successful there.'

'I left for personal reasons, Dr Saunders.'

Her voice was cool, distant even, so Daniel had no idea why the hairs on the back of his neck sprang to attention. He glanced at her CV again, needing a moment to collect himself. He hadn't felt this aware of a woman in a very long time, not since Camille, his wife, had died, in fact. That it should happen now, and with seemingly so little reason, surprised him. He cleared his throat.

'I see. So what attracted you to the post here at The Larches? You do understand that it's only temporary? Beth—Dr Andrews, that is—is planning to return once her maternity leave is over. Barring any unforeseen changes to her plans, she will be back at work next September.'

'I understand that. It was perfectly clear from your advertisement.' Eleanor Munroe pinned him with a chilly stare. 'I wouldn't have wasted your time or mine by applying for the post if I wasn't happy with the terms.'

'Quite so.' Daniel summoned a smile although he couldn't help feeling uncomfortable at the frosty rebuke. She certainly wasn't a pushover, he decided, storing that titbit away for future reference.

'Right, now we've established that, let me tell you about the practice,' he continued briskly, needing to take control of the proceedings once more. He wasn't normally indecisive when it came to his work—he was always single-minded and focused. However, Dr Munroe seemed to possess the ability to unsettle him and he wanted to get back on track. 'The Larches, whilst being a rural practice, is extremely busy, mainly because we cover such a wide area of the Yorkshire Dales. As you will know from our advertisement, as well as the main surgery here in Beesdale we run a branch surgery at Hemsthwaite. Between the two sites we have roughly four and a half thousand patients on our books. So if you thought it would be easier working here than in your previous post then I'm afraid you were mistaken.'

'I didn't apply for the job because I thought it would be the easy option,' Eleanor Munroe said brusquely. 'On the contrary, I am looking forward to being kept busy should I decide to accept the position.'

Daniel could feel his eyebrows rise and struggled to control them but Dr Munroe's confidence was more than a little startling. There had been no trace of doubt in her voice that she would be hired, no hint at all that she saw this interview as anything more than a formality. Eleanor Munroe obviously knew her own worth. And what was more, she intended to make sure that everyone else was aware of it too!

Ellie could feel perspiration trickling down her back. That had come out completely wrong! She knew it wasn't a given that she would be hired for the job. Despite first-class references and glowing endorsements, there were other factors to consider, the main one being that Dr Saunders needed to be sure they could work together. That seemingly arrogant statement would hardly have endeared her to him, would it? If she could have taken back the words she would have done so, but there was nothing she could do now except brazen it out.

Ellie sat up straighter, curbing the urge to run her hand over her newly short hair. She had never worn her hair so short before but she had decided to make a lot of changes to her life and changing her appearance had been first on her agenda. Once she had sorted out her new hairstyle, she had bagged up all the pretty, feminine dresses, the jewel bright tops, the high-heeled shoes, and given them to a charity shop. Her wardrobe now consisted of serviceable tailored trousers and shirts—neat, tidy, professional. Now that she was concentrating on what *she* wanted, she didn't need any more frippery.

'Well, there's no doubt that anyone who works here will be kept extremely busy,' Daniel Saunders said evenly, although Ellie could tell that her comment had been added to the minus column on her score sheet.

She bit back a groan, not wanting him to guess how mortified she felt. She wanted this job—no, not wanted it, *needed* it. If she moved to Yorkshire it would be the first step towards rebuilding her life. Maybe the future wasn't going to turn out the way she had thought it would but she intended to have a good life and on her terms too. Even though she'd been betrayed in the worst possible way, she was going to use what had happened to her advantage. She had always been a rather cautious person, preferring to stick to what she knew, but not any more. No, she intended to travel and see something of the world while she furthered her career. Maybe what had happened had been a blow but she would get over it. She was determined about that!

Ellie was so lost in her thoughts that it was a moment before she realised Dr Saunders had asked her a question. 'I'm sorry,' she said, feeling the embarrassed colour run up her neck. She hated to be caught unawares. She thrived on order and preferred to be prepared at all times. However, there was something about the man seated opposite that unsettled her.

'I asked if moving up here would create any problems for you, Dr Munroe.' Daniel Saunders shrugged, drawing Ellie's unwilling attention to the width of his shoulders. He was casually dressed in navy chinos and a light blue shirt with the sleeves rolled up to his elbows and, despite herself, Ellie couldn't help noticing how the blue of his shirt brought out the midnight blue of his eyes and highlighted the steel-grey streaks at his temples before she forced her mind away from such nonsense.

'Problems?' she repeated uncertainly. 'In which way, Dr Saunders?'

'You may need to consider someone else's views. It's a long way from Kent to Yorkshire and a lot of people might not be happy about relocating so far away.'

'I don't need to consider anyone else, I assure you.' Ellie sat up straighter, annoyed that he should have asked her a question like that. Maybe she should have let it go but, after what had happened recently, it stung. She glared at him. 'So if you're trying to find out if I have a husband or a partner who might object then I consider it a blatant infringement of my rights. I think you will find that no prospective employer has the right to discriminate against a female employee on such grounds.'

'I'm sure that's correct, Dr Munroe. However, to set your mind at rest, it's a question I would ask any potential employee. Male *or* female.'

His tone was as hard as flint and Ellie realised with a sinking heart that she had completely blotted her copybook now. No way was he going to offer her the job after this. Pushing back her chair, she stood up, wanting to bring the interview to a conclusion before she did something unforgivable. She hadn't cried, not even when she had found her fiancé in bed with one of their colleagues that day. She had held onto her composure throughout it all, right through the apologies and the ever more elaborate excuses. She hadn't even lost it when Michael had tried to blame *her* for his behaviour yet, for some reason, at that moment she could have stood there and wept.

'I apologise. I should never have said that. It was completely out of order. Thank you for seeing me, Dr Saunders. I hope you find someone suitable to fill the post.' Ellie swung round and headed towards the door. She knew it was directly behind her but she couldn't seem to see where she was going. She blundered into a filing cabinet and winced when the metal dug painfully into her hip. What was wrong with her? Why couldn't she find her way out?

'Here. Come and sit down.'

A large and surprisingly comforting hand closed around her arm as she found herself being led back to the chair. Ellie dropped down onto the seat because she really didn't have a choice. Tears were streaming down her face now, blinding her to everything else; she could only sit there while Daniel Saunders went to the sink and filled a glass with cold water.

'Drink this.' He crouched down beside her, so close that she could smell the clean fragrance of shampoo that clung to his hair. Holding the glass to her lips, he urged her to take a sip. A few drops of water trickled down her chin but before she could find a tissue, he wiped them away with his fingertips. 'Better?'

Ellie nodded, not trusting herself to speak. At any other time she would have been mortified by her loss of control but, oddly, she felt nothing. Daniel Saunders straightened up and put the glass on the desk then regarded her with eyes that held only compassion. He obviously wasn't the type to pass judgement, she thought, and found the idea strangely comforting.

'I apologise if I upset you, Eleanor. It wasn't my intention.'

His deep voice rolled softly over her name, affording it a surprisingly pleasing inflection. She had never really liked her name, had always thought it was too formal and old-fashioned. However, it sounded different when he said it, softer, gentler, far more appealing. She bit her lip, aware that she was allowing herself to be sidetracked. What did it matter how he said her name? The only thing that mattered was that she had made a fool of herself.

Pushing back the chair, she stood up, wanting to get away as quickly as possible. Maybe she had been pinning her hopes on getting this job but there would be other jobs in other parts of the country or abroad. Maybe she had promised her parents that she would stay in the UK until she had thought things through properly, but if she moved overseas, to Australia or New Zealand for instance, there would be no risk of her having to see Michael ever again…

'Right, it's time I gave you the conducted tour. We were lucky enough to secure funding to improve the facilities here so you may be surprised by what we offer our patients.' Daniel Saunders stepped around her and opened the door. His eyebrows rose when Ellie failed to move. 'Whenever you're ready, Eleanor.'

'Oh! But I thought…' Ellie tailed off, unsure what was happening. Why on earth was he offering to show her around when there was no chance of her being offered the job?

'You thought that you'd blown it?' Daniel Saunders laughed softly. 'On the contrary, Eleanor, it seems to me that you're exactly the sort of person I want working here.'

'I am? But why? I mean, I made a complete and utter mess of my interview, didn't I? And if that wasn't enough, I compounded my mistakes by breaking down and crying.' She shook her head. 'If I were in your shoes, Dr Saunders, I wouldn't hire me for all the tea in China!'

'It's Daniel. If we're going to be working together then I can't see any point in us standing on ceremony.' His blue eyes were filled with certainty when they met hers and Ellie felt a surge of warmth flow through her and start to melt the ice that had enveloped her these past terrible months. It was all she could do to concentrate as he continued in the same quietly assured tone.

'As for hiring you, from where I'm standing you seem like the ideal choice. I don't want someone working here who can't relate to our patients, someone who fails to understand that the problems life throws at them can and do impact on their health. I also don't want someone who's afraid to show her feelings either. So will you take the job, Eleanor? Please?'

CHAPTER TWO

'BASICALLY, WHAT I'D like you to do, Beth, is help her settle in. Every practice has its own way of doing things and I think it would help if Eleanor was shown the ropes rather than simply being thrown in at the deep end.'

Daniel leant back in his chair, wondering if his partner had any idea how important it was to him that Eleanor wasn't put under any pressure. Even though he couldn't understand why he felt this way, he knew that he wanted to make the move to The Larches as stress-free as possible for her. Maybe she had appeared supremely confident at the start of her interview but it had soon become clear that it wasn't the case. There was a vulnerability about Eleanor Munroe that had aroused all his protective instincts.

'Of course.' Beth Andrews smiled at him. 'It

will be a big change for her, working here. Just basics, like the fact that we're almost an hour's drive from the nearest hospital, will be a challenge for her. We're far more hands-on when it comes to our patients than a lot of practices.'

'Exactly.' Daniel breathed a little easier when Beth gave no sign that she considered his request strange. Maybe it wasn't either, he mused. After all, if Eleanor was unable to do the job she had been hired for then it would impact on him. The last thing he wanted was to have to put in more hours at the surgery when Nathan was in his final year at sixth form college.

When Camille had died four years ago, his son had gone completely off the rails. He had dropped out of school and fallen in with a bad crowd too. Daniel had been afraid that Nathan would never get his act together but, after a lot of heartache, he'd come through. However, if Nathan was to achieve the grades he needed for university, he had to stay focused, and to do that *he* needed to be there to support him. Little wonder that he had been so worried about his new locum, was it?

The thought reassured him, helped to settle his mind. If he was honest he had felt more than a little concerned that Eleanor Munroe had occupied his thoughts so much lately. He had lost count of the times she had popped into his head and it was good to know why it had been happening.

'Thanks, Beth.' Daniel smiled as he pushed back his chair and stood up. 'I really appreciate it.'

'No problem.'

Beth grimaced as she levered herself up off the chair. She was eight months pregnant and Daniel guessed that she was finding it difficult to get around. He remembered how tired Camille had been when she had been expecting Nathan and she had stopped work well before this stage. However, as a soon-to-be single mother, Beth didn't have the luxury of leaving work early. She had opted instead to continue working and take the bulk of her maternity leave after her baby was born. Nevertheless, Daniel made a note to ask Marie, their head receptionist, to redirect as many of Beth's patients as possible to him. He didn't want Beth pushing herself too hard during her final week, neither did he want Eleanor being placed under too much pressure. It would be better if he took up the slack for now.

Once again Daniel found himself worrying how his new employee would fare. Oh, there was no doubt about her ability—her CV was proof of that. However, would she be able to deal with whatever had led her to leave her previous post? he found himself wondering as he made his way to Reception. Although he knew nothing about Eleanor on a personal level, instinct told him she had suffered some kind of major blow and recently too. Had she been let down in love, perhaps? Treated badly by some man?

Daniel was surprised by how angry the idea made him feel. Bearing in mind that he had met her only the once, and that it hadn't been the most auspicious of meetings either, it shouldn't have had this effect on him. Nonetheless, the thought of some guy hurting her made him feel extremely angry and it was completely out of character for him to react that way. His expression must have been unusually grim as he stopped at the reception desk because Marie looked at him in surprise.

'What's wrong?' she demanded. In her forties, with two grown-up sons, Marie had worked at The Larches ever since Daniel had taken over the practice and didn't believe in standing on ceremony. 'Has something upset you? Because I have to say that you could turn the milk sour with a face like that!'

'Sorry.' Daniel dredged up a smile. Admitting that he was upset at the thought of their new locum being unlucky in love would have caused no end of questions, most of which he couldn't have answered even if he'd wanted to. He swiftly changed the subject because he really and truly didn't want to start searching for explanations at that moment. 'I know it's short notice, but can you redirect as many of Beth's patients as possible to me? I don't want her tiring herself out by doing too much in her last week.'

'Of course. But what about the new doctor? What's her name again? I wrote it down somewhere...'

'Eleanor Munroe,' Daniel said promptly, and felt a little thrill course through him as her name rippled off his tongue. He glanced at the clock above the desk, needing a moment to collect himself. The last thing he wanted was Marie suspecting how he felt. 'She should be here any minute...'

'Good morning.'

Daniel swung round when he recognised Eleanor's voice. In a fast sweep his eyes ran over her from the severely styled hair to the sensible shoes on her narrow feet and he felt his nerves start to tingle. What was it about this woman that affected him so much? he wondered dizzily. As an eligible widower, he'd had his share of women pursuing him over the past four years. However, he had never taken them up on their invitations to lunch and dinner, or whatever else had been on offer. The fact was that he hadn't been interested in them.

Not once had he felt that spark, that flicker of desire ignite inside him, yet as he looked at Eleanor, he felt it now. And in a big way too. Why it was happening was a mystery but he couldn't lie to himself, couldn't pretend that he didn't feel it. He was attracted to her and it couldn't have come at a worst time either. If she had been let down, as he suspected, the last thing she needed was to embark on another relationship, especially with him. He didn't have time for a relationship. He needed to focus on Nathan: his son's future *had* to take priority over everything else.

Daniel took a deep breath, clamping down on the surge of disappointment that rose inside him. There was no question about what he was going to do. He was going to ignore all these crazy feelings and be there for Nathan.

Ellie could feel her tension mounting as Daniel continued to stare at her without uttering a word. Was he having second thoughts? she wondered anxiously. Regretting whatever impulse had led him to offer her this job?

She bit her lip, unsure what she was going to do if that proved to be the case. She had given up the lease on the flat in Kent, sold all her furniture, and got rid of everything that reminded her of Michael. One of the main attractions about this job was the fact that it came with accommodation. There was a furnished flat above the surgery, which had seemed like a godsend. However, if she lost the job then it was going to be extremely difficult to start all over again. She had been living off her savings for the past months but they certainly wouldn't stretch to cover the costs of renting a flat and furnishing it. The prospect of not only having to find herself another job but somewhere to live as well was daunting to say the least.

Ellie breathed in deeply when she felt her eyes prickle with tears. Since her interview, she had found herself breaking down all too often. It was as though Daniel's kindness that day had opened the floodgates and all the hurt she had held at bay kept flooding out. However, there was no way that she intended to break down again in front of him. He might think she was playing the sympathy card and that was the last thing she wanted.

'Hi, Eleanor. Nice to meet you. I'm Marie, the head receptionist and general factotum around here.' The middle-aged woman behind the desk leant over and offered Ellie her hand.

'Good to meet you too,' Ellie replied automatically, shaking hands. She glanced at Daniel, wishing he would say something. If he was having second thoughts, it would be better if he said so rather than standing there, looking at her…

'Sorry.' Daniel suddenly roused himself. He smiled apologetically as he offered her his hand. 'I was wool-gathering. Welcome to The Larches, Eleanor. It's good to have you on board.'

Ellie felt relief wash over her as she reached for his hand. She had completely misread the situation, it appeared. Daniel wasn't thinking of rescinding his offer after all. His hand closed around hers and a frisson ran through her when she felt the strength of his fingers envelop hers. For some reason she couldn't explain, it felt right to have him hold her hand, right and wonderfully reassuring. Even though she knew nothing about him, she felt safe with him. Safe and cherished.

'It's good to be here,' she murmured, quickly withdrawing her hand. She dredged up a smile, needing to rid her head of such nonsense. Daniel Saunders was her employer, no more and no less than that. He wasn't going to have any impact on her life outside work.

'So where would you like to start? I imagine you'd like to see the flat first.' Daniel's voice held no trace of anything yet Ellie felt herself flush when he addressed her. It was so unlike her to react that way that she found herself stammering.

'I...ahem... Whatever suits you best, Dr Saunders.'

'It's Daniel,' he reminded her, his blue eyes holding hers fast for a moment before he turned away. 'Maybe we can leave the flat till later then. I've had a word with Beth and she's going to show you the ropes so you can get an idea of how we do things around here.'

'I'm sure that won't be necessary,' Ellie said swiftly, wanting to put an end to the pleasantries. The sooner she got down to work, the more comfortable she would feel. It was the newness of it all that was unsettling her, of course, not Daniel per se. It was a relief to have found an explanation and she hurried on. 'I've been a GP for some time now and I'm completely up to speed when it comes to all the paperwork and everything else that comes with the job.'

'I'm sure you are. However, every practice has its own way of doing things and The Larches is no different, so I'd appreciate it if you would indulge me on this point.' He smiled thinly, making Ellie wish that she hadn't said anything. The last thing she wanted was him thinking that she was someone who made a fuss.

'Of course. I… I just didn't want to waste Dr Andrews's time,' she explained lamely. 'I'm sure she must be very busy.'

'She is.' Daniel placed his hand under her elbow as he led her away from the desk.

Ellie drew in a quick breath, trying to stem the nervous fluttering of her heart, but it refused to quieten down. It was as though Daniel's touch had set off a chain reaction, ripples of awareness flowing from where his fingers lightly gripped her arm and spreading throughout her entire body. It was hard not to show how alarmed she felt when he stopped and looked at her.

'However, between you and me, Eleanor, I'm trying to cut down the amount of work Beth is doing. She's eight months pregnant and this is her last week in work before she goes on maternity leave, so I don't want her overdoing things and making herself ill. If she's showing you the ropes, at least I know that she isn't rushing around all over the place.'

'Oh, right. I see.' Beth carefully withdrew her arm, stifling a wholly ridiculous feeling of disappointment. Of course Daniel was more concerned about his long-time colleague than he was about her!

'I knew you'd understand.' Daniel treated her to a strangely intimate smile before he led the way along the corridor. He stopped at one of the doors, tapping lightly on the beechwood panels before opening it. 'Beth, I've got Eleanor with me. If you can show her how we do things, as we discussed, that would be great.' He gestured for Ellie to step forward, winking at her as she passed him. Ellie felt a rush of warmth engulf her. It was as though they were two conspirators sharing a secret and she had to admit that she rather liked the idea. She was smiling when she stepped into the room and the pretty, fair-haired woman seated behind the desk smiled back.

'Hi, Eleanor. It's good to meet you. Come on in and make yourself comfortable.' She chuckled, her hazel eyes filled with mischief as she glanced at Daniel. 'This is going to be your room next week, so it will give you a chance to try it out for size. Anything you don't like tell the boss. I'm sure he'll do *everything* possible to sort it out!'

'Don't go putting ideas into Eleanor's head,' Daniel retorted. 'She'll be giving me a list of things she wants before I know it.' He rolled his eyes. 'Like that singer who demanded a basket of kittens to play with in her dressing room before she would go on stage and perform!'

'Oh, you don't need to worry about finding me any kittens,' Ellie said, completely deadpan. She waited a beat then grinned at him. 'I much prefer puppies!'

Everyone laughed, Eleanor included, and it was such a shock that she found it hard to believe what was happening. She couldn't remember the last time she had laughed, couldn't recall when she had felt so light-hearted. Ever since that dreadful day when she had found Michael and Stacey together, her world had been filled with darkness, but all of a sudden it felt as though the gloom had lifted and it was all thanks to Daniel. Even if they were destined to be no more than colleagues, Ellie knew that she would be grateful to him for ever for that.

The morning flew past. Ellie was surprised by how differently things were done at The Larches. Although there were all the usual forms to fill in, the surgery offered a range of services to its patients that hadn't been available on-site where she had worked before. She mentioned it to Beth when they stopped to drink the coffee Marie had made for them.

'It's all down to our location,' Beth explained, blowing on the hot liquid to cool it. 'It takes almost an hour to reach the nearest hospital on a good day and far longer than that if the weather's bad. A lot of patients both here at The Larches and at Hemsthwaite can't undertake that kind of a journey. That's why Daniel fought so hard to secure funding to provide more facilities on site.'

'So what else do you offer?' Ellie asked as Beth paused to sip her coffee. 'You said that several consultants from the hospital hold clinics here— did you mention something about a dentist as well?'

'Yes. That's right. We have an arrangement with a dental practice—they see patients here once a week. The same goes for the optician—patients can make an appointment to see him here on a Wednesday,' Beth explained and grimaced. 'Dratted Braxton Hicks contractions. They woke me up this morning. I was not pleased either as it was the first time I hadn't had to get up through the night to go to the loo.'

'What a nuisance,' Ellie said sympathetically. 'Daniel said that you only have a few weeks before your baby is due.'

'Hmm, three, although first babies are notoriously late.' Beth wriggled around, trying to get comfortable, and Ellie frowned.

'Are you sure they're Braxton Hicks? You do seem to be in a lot of discomfort.'

'Oh, I'm sure it will pass,' Beth said, levering herself up off the chair. She let out a gasp as water suddenly gushed out from between her legs.

'I doubt it!' Ellie exclaimed, jumping to her feet. Putting her arm around Beth's waist, she helped her to the couch and got her settled. 'It looks as though it's the real thing so let's get you out of those wet undies and have a look. If your waters have broken then it won't be long before your baby's on its way too.'

'I can't believe this!' Beth exclaimed, wriggling out of her sodden underwear. 'I should have another three weeks before the baby arrives.'

'It's easy to get confused about the dates,' Ellie said soothingly, lifting Beth's skirt so she could examine her.

'But I'm not confused. I know exactly when I got pregnant. It was the night before Callum went away. It couldn't have happened any other time because we hadn't spoken let alone made love for almost a year before that!'

'Oh.' Ellie wasn't sure what to say, and Beth sighed.

'Callum and I split up last year. We'd been try-ing for a baby for the best part of three years—ever since we got married, in fact—but it just didn't happen.' Her voice echoed with pain and Ellie's heart went out to her.

'It must have been difficult for you,' she said quietly.

'It was. We tried fertility treatment but it didn't work, and in the end the constant pressure of hop-ing that this time we'd get lucky proved too much.' Beth bit her lip. 'Callum told me that he couldn't handle it any more and that he wanted a divorce.'

'I'm so sorry,' Ellie said sincerely. 'It must have been awful for you both, although surely it made a difference when you found out you were preg-nant?'

'I was thrilled, thrilled and shocked that it should have happened right out of the blue like that. As for Callum, well, I've no idea how he feels, although I can guess.' She laughed harshly. 'I wrote to tell him I was pregnant, you see, but he's never bothered to reply. I think that says it all, doesn't it? No, this baby's my responsibility and no one else's.'

She broke off as another contraction began. Ellie frowned, wondering how she would have reacted in similar circumstances. She sighed because the likelihood of her having found herself in the same position was zero. Michael had been fanatical about making sure she didn't get pregnant. At the time, Ellie had thought it was because he had wanted to do the right thing, make sure they were married before they embarked on parenthood. Now she wasn't so certain any more. Had Michael been desperate to avoid her getting pregnant so that it wouldn't impact on him?

It was something Ellie knew she needed to think about but not right now. Now she needed to focus on Beth and the baby. She waited until the contraction had passed then examined Beth again. 'You're already about six centimetres dilated so your baby's definitely going to make his appearance very soon.'

'Oh, no!' Tears filled Beth's eyes. 'It's too early! I couldn't bear it if something went wrong now. I've waited so long for this child.'

'Nothing is going to go wrong,' Ellie assured her, mentally crossing her fingers that she wasn't tempting fate. Delivering Beth's baby wouldn't have posed a problem if they'd been in a fully equipped maternity unit. However, after what she had learned about the nearest hospital being an hour's drive away, she couldn't help feeling anxious. She summoned a smile, determined not to let Beth know that she was worried. 'Now can you tell me what arrangements you've made for the birth? I take it that you're booked into the maternity unit with it being your first child.'

'That's right.' Beth made an obvious effort to calm herself. 'I wanted to have the baby at home but Polly talked me out of it. She said it would be safer if I had it in the hospital seeing as I'm a first-time mum and that bit older too.'

'And who's Polly?' Ellie asked, needing to be clear about the details.

'She's the local midwife—Polly Davies,' Beth explained. 'I've been seeing her for my antenatal check-ups. In fact, I saw her only last Friday.'

'And what did she say?' Ellie asked.

'Oh, that everything was fine—blood pressure, baby's heartbeat, et cetera.' Beth frowned. 'She did say that the baby seemed to be quite low down, now I think about it.'

'Probably getting ready to make his exit,' Ellie said, laughing.

'Probably. The little rip!'

Beth laughed as well and Ellie was relieved to see that she appeared far less anxious. Good. The last thing she wanted was for Beth to be uptight if they had to deliver the baby here. The thought helped her focus on what needed to be done and she squeezed Beth's hand. 'I'll go and phone the hospital and let them know what's happening. I'll also get hold of Polly. With a bit of luck, she'll be able to lend a hand here. I'll be as quick as I can. OK?'

Beth nodded, her face screwing up as another contraction began. Ellie hurried from the room and made straight to Reception, knowing that Marie would have all the phone numbers. She was dealing with a patient and Ellie waited until she had finished. Lowering her voice so it wouldn't carry across the waiting room, she quickly explained what was going on.

'Really!' Marie's mouth dropped open. 'But she's another three weeks to go. Are you sure it isn't a false alarm?'

'Quite sure,' Ellie said firmly. 'This baby is definitely on its way and there's nothing we can do to stop it. Can you phone the hospital and let them know? We'll need an ambulance, although I doubt if it will get here before the big event.'

'Of course.' Marie picked up the phone, although she still appeared slightly stunned.

'Oh, and can you get hold of Polly too? Apparently, she's been responsible for Beth's antenatal care. It would be a huge help if she could give me a hand.'

'I'll phone her first,' Marie promised. 'She lives in town so she can be here in no time.'

'That's great. Thanks.' Ellie started to turn away then paused. 'Daniel needs to know what's going on. Which is his room again?'

'First door on the right,' Marie explained, then turned her attention to the phone. 'Polly, it's Marie. You won't believe what's happened…'

Ellie left the receptionist to make the calls and hurried back to Beth, pausing en route to tap on Daniel's door. She popped her head into the room when he bade her to enter. 'I'm sorry to disturb you,' she said, smiling apologetically at the young woman holding a fractious toddler on her knee. 'But can I have a quick word?'

'Of course.' Daniel excused himself and stepped out into the corridor. He frowned. 'There's nothing wrong, I hope. I thought Beth was showing you around.'

'She was but we've hit a snag.' Ellie felt decidedly awkward about interrupting him during a consultation but there was really nothing else she could have done in the circumstances.

'A *snag*?' he echoed in a voice that hinted at displeasure. 'What are you talking about?'

Ellie's mouth compressed, not enjoying the fact that he obviously thought she was being a nuisance. She prided herself on her self-sufficiency and it stung to realise that he thought she was the type of person who needed constant support.

'Beth's baby is coming,' she explained coldly. She raised her hand when he went to speak. 'No, there's no doubt about her being in labour. Marie is arranging for an ambulance and phoning Polly to see if she can come and help. I thought you should know, although I apologise for disturbing you.'

With that she turned away, making herself walk steadily along the corridor even though in truth she felt like running off and hiding. She bit her lip when she felt the far too ready tears spring to her eyes. Maybe it hurt to have Daniel speak to her so sharply but she could live with it. After all, he was her boss, nothing more. It didn't matter how he spoke to her so long as he wasn't rude.

It all sounded so sensible in theory but as she

opened the door, Ellie realised that it did matter, that it mattered a great deal. For some reason she wanted Daniel to speak to her with warmth and make her feel that she was valued. How pathetic was that!

CHAPTER THREE

DANIEL COULD HAVE bitten off his tongue for speaking so sharply to Eleanor. If it weren't for the fact that he had a patient waiting, he would have gone after her and apologised. Taking a deep breath, he went back into the room and sat down.

'I apologise for the interruption, Mrs Walsh,' he said to the woman seated in the chair. 'You were about to explain how you hurt your arm.'

'I… I tripped, Dr Saunders. Over…ahem…one of Alice's toys.'

The young woman ran a trembling hand over her daughter's wispy blonde hair. Although both mother and child were neatly dressed in expensive outfits, there was something not quite right about their appearance. The little girl's hair looked as if it hadn't been brushed and yet Madeleine Walsh had taken the time to apply a heavy layer of make-up. Daniel leant across the desk, using the excuse of reaching for Mrs Walsh's file while he examined her face more closely. Was that a bruise he could see on her cheek? And another on her neck?

'I see,' he said, sitting back in his seat. He smiled at her, although he had a bad feeling about this. It wasn't the first time that Madeleine Walsh had come to see him after a supposed fall; this was her third visit in the last six months. Although he hadn't noticed any sign of bruising then, it could be because he hadn't been looking for it. He needed to get to the bottom of this situation and soon. 'Did you hurt yourself anywhere else apart from your arm? Your face looks bruised to me—did you bang it?'

'Oh…erm…yes, I must have done.' The woman put her hand to her cheek and Daniel could see the fear in her eyes. 'I'm ever so clumsy,' she muttered. 'Always tripping up and banging into things.'

'Easily done,' Daniel said evenly. 'As long as you're sure that it was an accident. Anything you tell me won't go any further, Mrs Walsh, I assure you.'

'Of course it was an accident!' the woman declared, flushing. 'I tripped over one of Alice's toys—one of her dolls, actually—and fell down the stairs. I… I must have put out my hand to save myself and that's how I hurt my arm.'

'Let me take a look.' Daniel got up and came around the desk. Crouching down, he went to examine her arm, stopping when little Alice shrank away from him. 'It's all right, poppet,' he said softly. 'I just want to look at Mummy's arm so I can make it better.'

'She's not good with strangers,' Madeleine Walsh said hurriedly, cuddling the trembling child to her.

'Does she attend the nursery school?' Daniel asked levelly, although the bad feeling he had was growing worse by the second. Alice was four years old and in his experience most children her age had got over their shyness and were happy to socialise with people outside the family unit.

'No. I decided not to send her.' Madeleine Walsh

bit her lip then rushed on. 'She's very shy and it didn't seem right to send her to a place where I know she'll be unhappy.'

'She'll have to go to school next year, though, won't she?' Daniel pointed out, gently examining the woman's arm. The wrist was swollen and heavily discoloured. It was obviously painful because Mrs Walsh gasped when he touched it. 'Sorry. I can tell how painful it is, although I can't say if it's broken or badly sprained. Can you move your fingers?'

'Yes.' Madeleine grimaced as she wriggled her fingers the tiniest bit. 'It's really painful, though.'

'It will be.' Daniel sat down again. 'I'm afraid it really needs X-raying to establish if it's broken or not. Is there anyone who can drive you to the hospital, your husband perhaps?'

'No, Nigel's in court this morning and I don't want to bother him,' Madeleine Walsh said quickly. 'Can't you put a bandage on it, Dr Saunders? I'm sure it's not broken and just needs some support while it heals. I wouldn't have bothered you if I could have done it myself.'

'I really think it needs to be X-rayed,' Daniel insisted. 'If it is broken then the last thing you want is for it to set badly and end up with a deformed wrist. If you don't want to contact your husband then I can arrange for someone to drive you to the hospital. We have a team of volunteers who very kindly ferry people there and back in situations like this.'

'Oh, I don't know… I've no idea what Nigel would say about that.' She looked so stricken that Daniel almost wished he hadn't suggested it. However, it was vital that she have her wrist X-rayed to avoid any future problems.

'I'm sure he will take the sensible view and be pleased that you got it attended to. I'll phone Mrs Goodison and see if she's free. She used to be a teacher at the junior school and she's very nice,' he added encouragingly as he reached for the phone.

'But what about Alice?' Madeleine Walsh protested. 'There's no one to look after her and I can't leave her.'

'You can take Alice with you. I know for a fact that Mrs Goodison has a child seat in her car—

she has grandchildren, you see. She'll be more than happy to look after Alice while you have the X-ray done too.'

Daniel made the call, not wanting to give Madeleine Walsh any more opportunities to wriggle out of the hospital visit. Fortunately, Barbara Goodison immediately agreed to run Mrs Walsh to the hospital and bring her back again afterwards. Once he had explained to Madeleine that she would be collected from home, he saw her out. He intended to follow up the case and find out if he was right to suspect that the woman was being abused by her husband. He didn't know Nigel Walsh personally as the man had never been to the surgery since the family had moved to Beesdale just over a year ago. However, from what he had heard Walsh was very high up in legal circles.

Daniel sighed as he went to ask Marie if she would wait a few minutes before sending in his next patient. Sadly, social standing had no bearing on that type of behaviour. It crossed all boundaries. Had Eleanor been a victim of abuse? It was obvious that something awful must have happened to her, something so bad that she had left her job and relocated to a different part of the country. His hands clenched. The thought of Eleanor suffering such treatment was more than he could bear.

'You're doing great,' Ellie said encouragingly as Beth breathed her way through another contraction. She checked her watch, frowning when she realised how close together the contractions were coming. It was obvious that the baby was going to be born very soon and she couldn't help feeling anxious. It was several years since she had delivered a baby during her rotations and it had been in the safety of a modern maternity unit with a couple of experienced midwives standing by. The thought of delivering Beth's baby by herself was decidedly scary. According to Marie, Polly was on her way back from one of the local farms and would get there as soon as she could; however, it seemed to be taking her an awfully long time. Ellie looked round when the door opened, hoping it would be her, but her hopes were dashed when

Daniel came into the room. Even though she could do with some support, she wasn't sure if she was glad to see him after their run-in earlier.

'How are we doing in here?' he asked as he came over to the couch. He smiled at Beth. 'Not quite how you planned it, I imagine.'

Beth laughed then grimaced as another contraction began. Daniel turned to Ellie, his mouth still curved into a smile, and she felt some of her unease dissipate. Surely he wouldn't smile at her like that if he was still annoyed with her?

'I'm sorry about before. I didn't mean to snap at you. Suffice to say that I was worried about the patient who was with me, not that it's any excuse.'

'It's all right,' Ellie said quickly, not wanting him to suspect how thankful she felt. She hated being in the wrong and had always done so ever since she was a child. Oh, she knew what lay behind it—she had worked that out a long time ago. Learning that she was adopted had made her aware of how different she was from Gemma, their parents' natural daughter. Gemma hadn't needed to be on her best behaviour all the time to earn their love; she hadn't needed to be kind or considerate because their parents would always adore her. Gemma, with her golden curls and laughing blue eyes, was the child they had longed for whereas Eleanor, with her straight black hair and solemn demeanour, had been the cuckoo in the nest.

Ellie pushed the thought to the back of her mind. She wasn't a child any more and she didn't need anyone's adoration to prove her worth. 'The contractions are coming roughly two minutes apart now. Do you know how long it will be before Polly gets here? Marie said she was on her way back from Outhwaite Farm.'

'Oh!' Daniel grimaced. 'It's the farm that's probably furthest away from here. It'll take Polly a good thirty minutes to get back, I expect, but I'll go and check where she is.' He strode to the door then paused to glance back. 'I meant what I said, Eleanor. I didn't mean to snap at you.'

He didn't wait for her to answer and Ellie was glad. She turned to Beth after he left, forcing down the bubble of happiness that had risen up inside her. She didn't need Daniel's approbation any more than she needed to be adored, she told herself sternly, but to very little effect.

She sighed. It had taken her a long time to develop a sense of her own worth. Growing up, she had always felt second-best compared to Gemma. Although her parents had been unfailingly kind and supportive, they had found it impossible to hide their delight in their natural daughter. Gemma had been so pretty and precocious and everyone had adored her—or so it had seemed to Ellie. Ellie had faded into the background after Gemma was born when Ellie was eight years old. It was only when she went to university that she had come into her own—made her own circle of friends, had her first boyfriend. She had slowly gained confidence and, once she had qualified and started practising, she had forgotten about the disappointments of her childhood. When she had started dating Michael Ross, another of the doctors at the practice where she'd worked, and had become engaged to him, her life had felt complete. And then she had let herself into his flat that morning and found him in bed with Stacey Roberts, one of the practice nurses, and her world had fallen apart...

'Ooh!'

Beth's groan brought Ellie back to the present. Bending down, she checked what progress they were making, her heart racing when she discovered that the baby's head was crowning. 'You're almost there,' she told Beth, trying to inject a note of confidence into her voice. 'Baby's head is crowning so it won't be long now.'

'The sooner the better,' Beth muttered through gritted teeth. Her face screwed up as another contraction began and Ellie quickly gathered together everything she would need once the baby was born. Fortunately, they had birthing kits in the supply cupboard so she put on a pair of gloves and placed everything close to hand—scissors to cut the cord, a soft cloth to dry the infant, some narrow tubing to clear its airway if it was necessary. The head was emerging now and she slid her hand beneath it, gently supporting its weight as first one shoulder and then the other followed.

'One more push should do it,' she told Beth, thanking her stars that Beth was so clued up about what to do. 'Here we go!'

The baby slithered out, screaming lustily, which was more than Ellie could have hoped for. It was a little girl, slightly on the small side, but absolutely perfect in every respect. Ellie wiped the mucus off the little one's face, smiling as she wrapped her in a towel and handed her to Beth. 'Congratulations. You have a beautiful little daughter.'

'A girl!' Beth exclaimed as she took her first look at her daughter. 'I was convinced I was having a boy!'

'Not disappointed, are you?' Ellie teased her.

'No way! She's gorgeous.' Beth dropped a kiss on her baby's head.

Ellie turned away when she felt her eyes fill with tears. She had always dreamed of having a child of her own. Maybe it had become even more important because she and the baby would have been related by blood and that would have been even more special. Now the dreams she'd harboured had been bagged up and disposed of along with all that unwanted clothing. She wouldn't have a child now because the last thing she planned to do was to fall in love again and risk being let down a second time. It hurt to know how much she would miss because of what had happened.

'Well, it looks as though you've managed fine without me!'

Ellie swung round when the door opened to admit a tall, red-haired woman. Taking a quick breath, she hurriedly composed her features into a welcoming smile. Maybe her life wasn't going to turn out how she had hoped it would but she would make the best of it. 'I take it that you're Polly,' she said, holding out her hand. 'I'm Eleanor Munroe, the new locum.'

'Polly Davies.' Polly shook hands then went over to Beth, smiling as she looked at the baby. 'What a little poppet! And not a bad size too considering you had another three weeks to go.'

'She's gorgeous, isn't she?' Beth murmured, stroking the baby's wrinkled little cheek.

'Oh, so it's a girl?' Polly laughed, her pretty face lighting up with amusement. 'That's ten pounds you owe me.' She looked round, deliberately drawing Ellie into the conversation. 'Beth was convinced she was having a boy but I was equally sure it would be a girl so we had a bet on it. Looks as though I'm the winner!'

'We're both winners,' Beth corrected her, laughing.

Ellie laughed as well but she couldn't pretend that her heart wasn't heavy at the thought of never having children of her own. It was hard to rid herself of the thought as she helped Polly deliver the afterbirth then get Beth and the baby ready for the transfer to hospital. Although Beth was reluctant to go, Polly managed to persuade her that it would be in her and the baby's best interests. By the time Daniel led in the paramedics, everything was ready.

'Let me know if they keep you in, Beth,' he said, planting a kiss on his partner's cheek. 'We'll set up a rota—that way you won't be inundated by everyone wanting to visit at the same time.'

'That would be great.' Beth's voice caught as she looked at the baby nestled in her arms. 'It'll be nice for this little one to have all her aunties and uncles there for her, even if her father isn't interested.'

Ellie stepped aside as the paramedics wheeled Beth and the baby out to the ambulance. Polly was following on by car and she left as well. Daniel sighed as he watched them go.

'I can't believe that Callum doesn't want anything to do with his own child, but he's never even bothered to contact Beth since she wrote to tell him she was pregnant.'

'So she said,' Ellie said quietly. 'It must be very difficult for her.'

'It must. It's hard enough bringing up a child on your own when it's the result of circumstances beyond your control, but it must be much worse when it's because the other parent doesn't want to be involved.'

There was real regret in Daniel's voice and Ellie found herself wondering if he was speaking from experience. She knew nothing about his personal life, whether he was married and had a family or what. However, before she could attempt to find out, he made an obvious effort to collect himself.

'Anyway, leaving all that aside, I wanted to thank you, Eleanor. Talk about being thrown in at the deep end!' He laughed ruefully. 'And here was I, trying not to put too much pressure on you!'

CHAPTER FOUR

DANIEL COULD HAVE bitten off his tongue when he saw Eleanor's face tighten. That she hadn't appreciated the comment was obvious and he couldn't blame her. No one liked to be made to feel that they weren't up to doing the job they had been hired for. He desperately wanted to explain but how could he when it would mean admitting that he had been worried about her, that he cared?

'Right. Better get back to work or the patients will think we've gone on strike. Any problems, buzz me.'

He swung round, not giving her a chance to say anything as he headed back to his room. Maybe he was taking the coward's way out but the thought of confessing how much she had been in his thoughts lately was out of the question. Maybe she did have issues that still affected her but he doubted if she would appreciate his concern. From what he had learned, Eleanor preferred to keep her own counsel and he would be well advised to remember that whenever he was tempted to interfere.

The morning flew past as it always did. They held open surgery each morning and they were always very busy. Although patients could make an appointment to be seen during the afternoon, Daniel had found that they preferred this system. Being a mainly rural community, it allowed more leeway for the farmers and their families. Livestock came first and people appreciated being able to visit the surgery when work allowed, rather than be tied to a set time and date. It was almost one by the time his last patient left so he tidied up and made his way to Reception. Marie had been joined by Lucy Burrows, who was doing her preregistration training in their on-site pharmacy. It was obvious that Marie had brought her up to speed about the morning's events.

'I can't believe that Beth has had her baby here!' Lucy declared when she saw Daniel.

'I know. It came as a bit of a shock, not least

of all to Beth,' Daniel replied, laughing. Lucy had been born and raised in Beesdale and had returned to the town after she had completed her degree. With a Master of Pharmacy degree to her credit, she could have moved anywhere in the country, but she loved the Dales and wanted to remain here.

'I wonder what she's going to call her,' Lucy continued, happily. 'Beth was convinced she was having a boy so she'll have to think of some girls' names, I imagine.'

'She will,' Daniel agreed, although he was only half listening. His ears had caught the sound of footsteps and he knew without needing to check that they belonged to Eleanor. How or why he was able to recognise them with such certainty, he had no idea, but he knew he was right and his heart seemed to beat a shade faster all of a sudden. It was an effort not to show how alarmed he felt as he turned to her. 'All done?'

He'd been aiming for lightness, for nonchalance, for...for *heaven knew what*, but he hadn't achieved it. No way! He inwardly winced when he realised how stilted he sounded. What made it worse was that out of the corner of his eye he saw Lucy and Marie exchange a look, confirmation, if he'd needed it, that he had messed up. All he could do was hope that Eleanor didn't know him well enough to realise how strangely he was behaving.

'Yes. Thank you.'

Daniel felt a jolt of shock hit him when he realised that Eleanor sounded the same as he did. Uptight. Stilted. *Aware*. His blood heated, gathering several degrees as it rushed through his veins. Eleanor was aware of him? Not just the normal sort of recognition of one human being for another but completely and totally aware of *him*? As a person? As a man? If his mind hadn't been already boggled it would have been so then. Daniel could barely get his head round the idea and definitely couldn't chase it away. It was a relief when Lucy unwittingly stepped into the breach.

'Hi, Eleanor, I'm Lucy Burrows. I'm doing my pre-reg training in the pharmacy. I also do a turn on the desk if we're pushed.'

'Nice to meet you, Lucy.' Daniel heard Eleanor take a quick breath and didn't know whether he felt relieved or sorry when he heard how normal she sounded. 'Actually, most people call me Ellie. I always think it sounds less, well, formal.'

Ellie. Daniel tried it out for size, oh, not out loud—he wasn't that far gone! It rolled around his tongue pleasantly enough yet for some reason it didn't feel quite right. He shot a glance at the woman standing beside him and felt his nerve endings start to fire out signals. Ellie was a pretty name, slightly more modern, a little more accessible, but it wasn't right for her: it didn't fit. He preferred Eleanor, preferred the sound of it, the feel of it, the sense of completeness. With Eleanor one got the whole woman. Whereas Ellie was just a fraction of the whole, the bits she wanted folk to see, not the bits she kept hidden. The bits, he realised, that *he* desperately wanted to get to know.

Ellie forced herself to respond as Lucy asked her how she had enjoyed her first morning at The Larches but it was an effort to concentrate. She had no idea what was going on in Daniel's mind but she could almost see the thought bubbles forming above his head. That he was thinking about her was a given and it was unsettling to say the least. It was a relief when the phone rang.

'I expect you're keen to see the flat. I've got the keys here so I'll take you up there now.' Daniel offered her a small bunch of keys that he'd taken from his pocket as they moved away from the desk.

'Thank you.' Ellie took them off him, trying to ignore how warm they felt from being tucked against his body. 'There's no need for you to come, though,' she said hurriedly, not sure she appreciated that idea. 'I'm sure you must have more important things to do. I can sort myself out.'

'It isn't a problem. Anyway, there are a couple of things I need to show you—how to work the boiler and where to find the stopcock, things like that.' He didn't give her time to protest any more as he led the way from the surgery, taking the path round to the rear of the building. 'The flat is completely self-contained,' he continued over his shoulder. 'Camille and I lived there when I took over the practice. We only moved out because of Nathan.' He laughed. 'We needed more space to fit in all his paraphernalia!'

'Oh. I see.' Ellie felt her heart sink. Although she knew it was silly, learning that Daniel was married and had a family was disappointing. She pushed that ridiculous thought to the back of her mind, determined that it wasn't going to set down roots. 'It must have been handy living on site, so to speak.'

'Yes and no.' Daniel paused so she could catch up with him. 'It was great not having to drive miles each day to get to work but the downside was that I was always on call. Folk knew exactly where to find me, day and night.'

'Mmm. I can see how that could be a problem,' Ellie agreed, frowning.

'You don't need to worry about that,' he said quickly. He put his hand on her arm and laughed. 'We've managed to train our patients now. They phone the out-of-hours number rather than hammer on the front door these days.'

He patted her arm then moved away but it was a moment before Ellie followed him. She could feel her arm tingling from where his hand had rested on it and had to resist the urge to rub it. Daniel had reached a flight of steps leading to the upper floor of the building and he paused again to wait for her.

Ellie forced her feet to move in his direction but inside she could hear alarm bells ringing. She was already far too aware of Daniel, more aware of him, in fact, than she had been of anyone before, including Michael. Her attraction to her ex had developed over time; it definitely hadn't been instantaneous as this had been. Was it the fact that she had suffered such a huge blow? she wondered. That being betrayed had left her vulnerable so that she had latched onto the first attractive man who had shown her any kindness?

Ellie wanted to believe it with a fervour that bordered on frenzy. Quite frankly, *any* explanation was better than thinking that this attraction she felt could develop into something more!

'And this is the main bedroom. The bed's new and so is the carpet. I decided to change them when I had the flat redecorated. The old ones were well past their use-by date.'

Daniel stepped back so that Eleanor could go ahead of him but she merely glanced into the room. Her eyes swept over the soft *café-au-lait-*coloured carpet and matching curtains and he found it impossible to decide if she liked what she saw or not. It had been the same with every room—a swift glance, a brief nod, and that had been it. Even though he knew it was ridiculous to feel even the tiniest bit miffed, he couldn't help it.

'So what do you think?' he said, trying to mask his disappointment. She wasn't to know how much effort he had expended getting the place ready for her. She had no idea that he had devoted a whole weekend just to choosing the colour for the walls or that buying new curtains had been such a nightmare—widths and lengths, patterned or plain—it had been like tiptoeing through a minefield! However, all the effort he'd expended wouldn't be worth a brass farthing if she didn't like it.

'I don't know what to say.'

She sank down onto the sofa and stared around

the bright and airy living room. He'd chosen sheer curtains for in here—well, he hadn't actually chosen them but had gone with what the sales assistant had advised—and he had been particularly pleased with the result. The view from the window was spectacular, the greens and mauves of the surrounding hills shown to advantage without heavy curtains to detract from it. But had he made an error of judgement? Would Eleanor have preferred something more substantial, more private?

'Look, I understand if you want to change things,' he said quickly. 'Don't think you have to live with what I've chosen...'

'I love it. The walls, the curtains. Everything.' She looked up and he could see tears shimmering in her eyes. 'I never expected this, Daniel. Thank you so much. It's perfect.'

'I'm glad you like it.' Daniel felt a lump come to his throat and had to swallow hard. He dredged up a rather rusty laugh. 'I had a horrible feeling that you loathed the place when you didn't say anything.'

'I was just overwhelmed.' She dashed away her

tears and smiled self-consciously. 'Sorry. I was expecting something fairly basic, you see, not this. This…well, this looks like a proper home.'

'Good. It's going to be your home for the next year, so I'm pleased you feel that way.' He took a deep breath, clamping down on the urge to tell her that it was her home for as long as she wanted it to be. Eleanor was here to cover Beth's maternity leave and once that was over she would leave. Better to get that clear in his head from the outset.

'Right then. Do you need any help?' he said, determined to get a grip on his thoughts. 'Those steps can be a real bind if you've got anything heavy to fetch up here, so I'll give you a hand.'

'Thank you but there's no need.' She stood up and he couldn't help noticing that her face had closed up again. 'I got rid of most of my things before I left Kent so there's nothing really heavy—just clothes and bedding mainly.'

'I see.' Daniel frowned, wondering why she had got rid of all her belongings. He longed to ask but some tiny shred of caution held him back. He had teetered on the very edge of that invisible line between colleagues but he hadn't crossed it. Yet. Once he did so there would be no going back and that wouldn't be wise. He had to concentrate on Nathan. He couldn't afford to involve himself in Eleanor's affairs. At the end of the day, his son came first.

Daniel's heart was heavy as he walked to the door. Maybe he was doing the right thing, but there was no denying that it felt as though he was abandoning Eleanor and the idea hurt him probably far more than it would have hurt her if she knew how he felt. Eleanor had no problem keeping to her side of that line.

'I'll leave you to it then. I've half a dozen home visits this afternoon so if you need anything, ask Marie.' He forced himself to smile, although it was an effort to appear upbeat. 'She's the fount of all knowledge and any problems, she can usually solve them.'

'I'll remember that.' Eleanor's voice was cool, proof, if he'd needed it, that she didn't feel anywhere near as confused as he did.

Daniel sketched her a wave and left. He went

back to the surgery and collected the list of calls that Marie had left for him. His first call was to one of the outlying farms so he got into his car and headed out of town. It was a good twenty minutes' drive there and that should give him time to get his thoughts together. Quite frankly, he couldn't understand why he was behaving this way. It wasn't as though he was desperate to have a relationship again, desperate to have sex. He hadn't slept with anyone since Camille had died, hadn't wanted to despite the fact that he'd had many opportunities. It was as though that side of him had died along with his wife and he had never imagined he would feel desire again.

Was that what he felt for Eleanor? Did he want to sleep with her? Yes, he did. However, deep down he knew that sex wasn't at the heart of this attraction he felt, that there was more to it than that, although he wasn't going to make the mistake of working out what that 'more' was. It was too risky when he needed to stay focused on Nathan.

Daniel's expression was grim as he turned in

through the farm gates. Meeting Eleanor couldn't have come at a worse time.

Ellie couldn't help feeling a deep sense of satisfaction as she switched off her computer. The day had gone much better than she had hoped. The patients she'd seen had been friendly and welcoming, genuinely grateful for her help. The other members of the team had also been highly supportive, going out of their way to make her feel at home. She knew she had made the right decision by applying for this job. It would help her get over what had happened, help her forget her disappointment and heartache. She just needed to concentrate on her work and everything would be fine.

'All finished?'

Ellie felt her heart lurch when the door opened and Daniel appeared. She hadn't seen him since he had shown her round the flat and she had forgotten the impact he had on her. Now, as she took stock of his rangy figure, she could feel that flicker of awareness shoot through her once more.

Was it just his looks that caused her to react this way? Or was it more than that, the air of kindness, of caring, of compassion he exuded?

She had been attracted to Michael initially because of his looks, although, if she was honest, it had taken a while to find anything attractive about his personality. Michael had very strong views on most matters and Ellie had had to reconcile herself to the fact that they didn't see eye to eye on a lot of subjects. Had that been a mistake? she wondered suddenly. Should she have compromised her views to accommodate his simply because she had been afraid of losing him?

'Eleanor?'

The concern in Daniel's voice brought her back to the present and Ellie jumped. 'Sorry, I was miles away. Yes, I'm all finished.'

'Good. I was hoping we'd be able to finish on time with it being your first day.' Daniel gave her a quick smile and she felt her heart flutter once more and fought to control it. This was ridiculous! She wasn't some infatuated teenager but a mature woman, a woman who knew what was what too.

'Well, it seems to have worked out that way,' she said lightly, standing up. She took her bag out of her drawer then glanced around, checking that the cupboard was locked and the tap wasn't running—all the itty-bitty jobs that she did automatically and yet for some reason seemed to have taken on a far greater importance with Daniel watching her...

'Humph!' She didn't realise that she had actually snorted in disgust at her behaviour until she saw his brows rise. Colour flooded her cheeks and she hurried to the door, praying that he couldn't read minds along with his other talents. Wanting to make a good impression on him was pathetic!

Ellie hurried along the corridor as though the hounds of hell were snapping at her heels. Marie looked up and grinned when she saw her approaching.

'Looks as though someone's eager to leave. It's not been *that* bad a day, has it?'

'No, of course not.' Ellie dredged up a smile but she was very aware that Daniel was standing right behind her. 'I just didn't want to hold you up. I'm not sure of the routine yet,' she added lamely.

'Oh, no fear of that.' Marie laughed. 'We're like a well-oiled machine. Aren't we, Daniel?'

'You could say that.'

His voice rumbled in Ellie's ear and she couldn't help herself: she shivered. It was as though the sound of his voice had seeped through every pore in her skin. She looked round and felt her breath catch when she found herself staring into his deep blue eyes. She could see her own reflection in them, tiny images of herself imprinted on the midnight-blue, and the shiver turned into a shudder. She had the craziest feeling that he was absorbing her very essence, drinking it in, making her part of him. And the scariest thing of all was that she wanted it to happen.

CHAPTER FIVE

A WEEK PASSED, then another, and life at The Larches settled back into its normal routine. Or, at least, on the surface it did. Daniel, however, was very aware of the difference it made having Eleanor there. Oh, it wasn't her work—he was more than happy with that. No, it was this feeling he had, this constant awareness of her being in the room next to his, and it was highly unsettling. He managed not to think about it when he was with a patient but as soon as they left, he found himself listening for any sign of her presence—a cough, the scrape of chair legs on the floor—*any* little thing at all.

In an effort to rid himself of such nonsense, he decided to do a stint at the Hemsthwaite surgery, using the excuse that it would benefit the staff as well as the patients if they all got to know one another better. Sandra Nelson, who worked there part time, was delighted at the thought of a change of scene. However, Bernard Hargreaves, the full-time member of staff, made it clear that he wasn't interested. Daniel suspected that Bernard was planning to retire shortly and didn't push him. It wouldn't benefit anyone if the older man was reluctant to take up the offer.

He spent a busy morning. With it being Monday, a lot of people had waited over the weekend before seeking medical attention. Daniel dealt with the usual sore throats and chesty coughs then saw a young man who had been brought into the surgery by his mother. Steven Applethwaite was seventeen years of age and attended the same college as Nathan. A tall, gangly young man with sandy hair, he looked pale and listless as he sat slumped in front of the desk.

'I had the devil of a job getting him here this morning, Dr Saunders, but he can't carry on the way he's been doing, that's for sure.' Mrs Applethwaite settled herself on the adjoining chair. A comfortably plump woman in her forties, she exuded an air of confidence. Daniel knew that the Applethwaites were a large farming family and guessed that Diane Applethwaite was used to taking charge.

'What exactly has been happening?' he asked, addressing the question to Steven.

'He's always tired no matter how much sleep he has,' Diane answered immediately. 'He stayed in bed most of the weekend but I still couldn't get him up this morning in time for college. It's as though he's got no energy.'

'Is that right, Steven?' Daniel asked neutrally. He held up his hand when Diane went to speak. 'If you wouldn't mind, Mrs Applethwaite, it would be better if Steven told me how he feels.'

Steven looked uncomfortable at being put on the spot. 'I just feel tired all the time, like Mum said,' he mumbled.

'Anything else?' Daniel prompted. 'Have you had a temperature or a sore throat, perhaps?'

'No.' Steven hesitated then rushed on. 'I feel thirsty all the time, though—I'm always drinking water and juice.'

'I see.' Daniel nodded. Getting up, he went to the cupboard and took out a sample jar. 'I'd like to check your urine, Steven. The bathroom's along the corridor to your left so can you go and pee in this for me and bring it back?'

Steven blushed right red as he took the jar. He was at an age when being asked to do such things caused him acute embarrassment. Diane Applethwaite looked Daniel straight in the eyes after her son disappeared.

'You think he's got diabetes, don't you, Dr Saunders?'

'I think it's a possibility, although I can't be sure until I've tested his urine,' Daniel explained carefully, not wanting to alarm the woman maybe unnecessarily.

'I should have realised it myself,' Diane said, shaking her head. 'Our Cathy—that's my sister— she's had diabetes since she was a girl. I remember her drinking pints of water before they found out what was wrong with her, but I never put two and two together.'

'It's easy to overlook things when you're busy.

And, let's be honest, teenaged boys aren't exactly forthcoming when it comes to any issues they have,' he added ruefully. 'I know from bitter experience how hard it is to get them to talk.'

'You're right there. I've got five lads and they're all very tight-lipped when it comes to anything personal,' Diane agreed. She sighed. 'Very different from the girls, they are.'

Steven came back just then and handed the specimen to Daniel. Daniel took it over to the worktop to test it. He nodded when the chemically coated strip showed an extremely high level of glucose. 'It's as I suspected, Steven. Your glucose level is far higher than it should be.' He came back and sat down. 'I'll need to do a blood test as well, but it appears that you may have diabetes mellitus.'

'That's what Auntie Cathy has, isn't it?' Steven said, turning to his mother. He went pale when she nodded. 'Does it mean I'll have to have injections like Auntie Cathy does?'

'Most probably,' Daniel confirmed, knowing what a shock it must be for the boy. He could imagine Nathan's reaction and tried to make the situation sound as positive as possible. 'However, if you do have to inject yourself with insulin you'll be shown what to do. After a while, it will just become part of your daily routine.'

'It's not routine, though, is it?' Steven said angrily, his eyes filling with tears. 'None of my friends have to inject themselves!'

'Perhaps they don't but they may have other health issues you know nothing about,' Daniel replied soothingly. However, his words had little effect as Steven leapt to his feet and rushed out of the room.

'I'm sorry, Doctor,' Diane said, getting up. 'He's always been a bit…well, sensitive. But that doesn't excuse his rudeness.'

'He's bound to be upset, Mrs Applethwaite. It's a lot to take in so please don't worry about it. The main thing now is to ensure he gets the appropriate treatment. I'd like him to do a fasting blood test, i.e. he's not to eat anything after his evening meal until blood is taken the following morning. It can be done here and if it confirms my suspicions then I'll refer him to the hospital.'

'I'll make sure he has it done,' Diane said staunchly.

'Good. Jessica will give you a leaflet explaining the procedure,' he told her, referring to one of the two practice nurses who covered both surgeries. 'She can also take the sample, although you can have it done at Beesdale if you'd prefer the phlebotomist to do it.'

'Here'd be better. It's a busy time at the moment—the sheep need bringing down from the hills before the weather turns and I'll be needed to lend a hand.' Diane sighed. 'Will Steven have to attend the hospital every week?'

'No. He will be seen by a specialist initially who will decide on a course of treatment for him. After that, he can be monitored here at the surgery. There's a monthly diabetes clinic, which the hospital staff run, so you won't need to be driving back and forth to town all the time.'

'Oh, that's a relief!' Diane exclaimed. 'Not that I'd have let Steven miss an appointment if he had needed to attend the hospital. But it will make life easier if he can be seen here.'

Daniel saw Diane out then buzzed in his next patient. The rest of the morning flew past and before he knew it, it was time for lunch. He exchanged the usual pleasantries with Bernard Hargreaves but he didn't linger. He was eager to get back to Beesdale to check what had been happening in his absence. He sighed as he got into his car. Why bother lying? Why not admit that he was eager to get back to see Eleanor?

It had been a busy morning but Ellie had enjoyed it. The range of problems she had dealt with had been very different from what she had encountered in her previous post. She knew that she was gaining valuable experience by working at The Larches, and that it would stand her in good stead when the time came to move on. Although she wouldn't be leaving for several months, she must never forget that she wasn't here on a permanent basis. It was a strangely depressing thought and she pushed it to the back of her mind as she left her consulting room. Sandra Nelson was just leaving Daniel's room and she greeted Ellie cheerfully.

'Been nice and busy, hasn't it?'

'It has.' Ellie returned her smile. She had taken an immediate liking to the older woman when they had met that morning. Sandra had a friendly and down-to-earth manner that had instantly put Ellie at her ease. 'So, have you enjoyed working here for a change?'

'I have, especially as I've had someone to talk to.' Sandra smiled conspiratorially. 'Bernard isn't one for chatting, let's just say. He prefers to get the job done and go home. I wouldn't be surprised if he handed in his notice soon. I get the impression he's looking forward to calling it a day and retiring.'

'Really?' Ellie frowned, wondering if it might be the opening she needed. If a post became vacant maybe Daniel would consider hiring her on a permanent basis, although she wasn't sure if it would be a good idea. Although she could learn a lot from working at The Larches, she was already far more aware of him than she should be. Would it really be wise to place herself in the position of seeing him day after day? She had sworn after she and Michael had parted that she wouldn't make the mistake of getting involved in a relationship again and she intended to stick to it.

'Would you consider applying for the post if Bernard does decide to leave?' Sandra asked, unconsciously latching onto Ellie's train of thought.

'I'm not sure,' Ellie replied. She shrugged when Sandra looked at her in surprise. 'I took this job knowing it was only temporary. I'm not sure if it's what I want to do long term, though.'

'Well, only you can decide that, although you could do a lot worse than work here. Isn't that right, Daniel?'

Ellie looked up in surprise, feeling her heart lurch when she saw Daniel standing by the reception desk. She hadn't seen him since the previous Friday and she found herself taking stock all over again. It was a chilly day, a brisk October wind giving a hint of what was to come, and he had dressed accordingly in a thick quilted coat that added bulk to his rangy figure. With his dark hair ruffled by the wind and his blue eyes sparkling, he was an arresting sight and Ellie couldn't stop staring at him. It was only when she realised that he had asked her a question that she dragged her thoughts together.

'Sorry. What was that?' she said hurriedly, willing the betraying colour not to flood her cheeks. She didn't want him thinking that he had an effect on her, even if it was true.

'I was just asking if you planned to stay in this part of the country,' he repeated.

'I... I'm not sure what my plans are yet,' Ellie said hastily. 'I may decide to move abroad. There are plenty of exciting opportunities for general practitioners in Australia and New Zealand.'

'There are indeed.' Daniel gave her a quick smile then turned to speak to Lucy Burrows, who was manning the desk that lunchtime.

Ellie headed for the door, not wanting anyone to suspect how hurt she felt. Oh, she knew it was stupid; after all, why should Daniel try to persuade her to stay in England? She was only here to cover Beth's maternity leave so why should he care where she went after that? And yet in some fragile corner of her heart she knew that it did matter, that it mattered a lot, and it worried her. She mustn't make the mistake of becoming dependent on Daniel, on thinking that his opinion counted. She had been down that road before with Michael and look how that had ended. The thought lent wings to her feet. Ellie had already left the building before Sandra caught up with her.

'Are you all right, love?' the older woman asked in concern. 'You dashed off as though the hounds of hell were after you!'

'Sorry.' Ellie drummed up a laugh, inwardly wincing when she realised how false it sounded. She rushed on, not wanting Sandra to guess how confused she felt. Maybe Daniel did have a strange effect on her but she wasn't prepared to alter her plans for him or any man. 'I skipped breakfast this morning and I'm absolutely ravenous. I can't wait to get something to eat!'

'I know the feeling!' Sandra laughed as well, accepting the excuse at face value. 'I'm on one of my never-ending diets and I'm always hungry. I even dream about food—how pathetic is that?'

'Poor you,' Ellie sympathised, although she couldn't help feeling guilty about the small white lie.

'Hmm, not what my hubby says when I wake him up, muttering about how many calories are in this or that delicious concoction.' Sandra grinned. 'Anyway, enough of my problems. I wanted to invite you to our autumn barbecue. We have one every year around this time as a kind of swan-song before everyone hunkers down for the winter. We're having it on the nineteenth this year, if you're free.'

'My birthday,' Ellie told her.

'Really? What a coincidence! So can you come or do you already have plans, with it being your birthday?'

'No, I've nothing planned,' Ellie admitted, refusing to think about the previous year and how she had celebrated with Michael. There was no point harking back to the days when it had felt as though she'd had the world at her feet.

'Great! Tim and I will look forward to seeing you then.' Sandra turned to leave then paused. 'If you want to bring anyone it's fine. The more the merrier, we always say.'

'Thank you,' Ellie replied, not wanting to admit that she had no one to bring. She went up to the flat after Sandra left and opened a can of soup and poured it into a bowl. Popping it into the microwave to heat up, she went to the window, wondering when she would stop measuring time by the things she had done with Michael. Was she still in love with him, even after the way he had treated her?

Closing her eyes, she tried to conjure up his face, something she had never had any difficulty doing before, but for some reason it didn't work this time. She could picture each feature separately—hazel eyes, light brown hair, a rather thin-lipped mouth—but they wouldn't coalesce into a whole no matter how she tried... Another face suddenly started to form and Ellie's breath caught. There was no need to force these features to take their rightful place. One minute there was nothing in her head except that jumble and the next there was Daniel. Whole. Complete. Unmistakable.

Ellie's eyes few open but the image stayed with her, etched into her mind so clearly that it seemed to belong there. Was it a sign? But a sign of what? That she was far too aware of him? She already knew that, didn't she? It was what she did with the knowledge that mattered now. If she was to avoid any more heartache then she had to stop what was happening and not allow it to progress any further.

If she could.

Daniel couldn't get the conversation he'd had with Eleanor out of his mind. *She was planning to move abroad after her contract here ended?* He knew that it shouldn't have mattered a jot what she chose to do, but it did. The thought of her moving thousands of miles away was like a heavy weight, pressing down on him. He longed to talk to her about her plans, even ask her to stay on at The Larches, but it wasn't up to him to interfere. He mustn't forget that he was simply her employer and nothing else.

The afternoon turned out to be as busy as the

morning, so they ended up running over time. Daniel offered to lock up so that Marie and the rest of the staff could get off home. Nathan played basketball on Monday evenings so he didn't need to rush home for once. He set the alarm then realised that Beth's keys to the surgery were hanging in the cupboard. Eleanor would need them to unlock the surgery. Daniel lifted them out, wondering if he should give them to her now or leave it until the morning. However, it would be typical if some kind of emergency happened and neither he nor Marie were available to open up. He would give them to Eleanor now and be done with it.

The wind was icy as he made his way round to the rear of the building. Although it was only the beginning of October, the weather was gearing itself up for winter. Winters in the Dales could be extremely harsh and definitely weren't to everyone's taste. Was that why Eleanor was thinking of moving overseas, so she could enjoy year-round sunshine? It would have been easy to accept that was the explanation, yet Daniel suspected that her reason for wanting to move abroad was linked to what had happened in the past. He frowned as he climbed the steps to the front door. Whatever it was, it must have been a particularly traumatic experience. Eleanor opened the door almost immediately when he rang the bell and Daniel could tell that she was surprised to see him.

'I'm sorry to bother you,' he said, clamping down on the thought as he held up the bunch of keys. When all was said and done, what business was it of his what she did? Nevertheless, he had to admit that he hated to think that she might move abroad for the wrong reasons. 'But I need to give you the surgery keys and explain how the alarm works. It would be absolutely typical if something happened and you needed to open up and didn't have any keys!'

'Oh. Right. You'd better come in then.' She led him into the living room, waving him towards a chair. 'I was just about to have a glass of wine,' she said, making an obvious effort to appear hospitable. 'Will you join me?'

'Better not.' Daniel shrugged. 'I've got to pick Nathan up in an hour's time. He's playing basketball,' he added, more for something to say than because he thought she would be interested. He was very aware that he was intruding on her free time. 'He plays for his college team and really enjoys it.'

'Nathan's your son?' She poured herself a glass of wine and sat down. 'How old is he?'

'Nineteen.'

'And he's still at college?' she queried, lifting the glass to her lips.

'Yes. He dropped out of school just before his GCSEs and missed over a year, so he's had to catch up,' Daniel explained, his eyes drawn to where her mouth touched the glass. She took a sip of wine then lowered the glass but his gaze remained locked on her mouth. There was the faintest sheen of moisture on her lips now and he felt his senses reel. Would her lips taste of wine? Would their sweetness be all the more potent if he kissed her?

'Was he ill?'

'Sorry?' Daniel forced his eyes away from her mouth, but he could feel the blood racing through his veins. The thought of kissing her and savouring the wine-sweet temptation of her lips was irresistible. When was the last time he had felt this kind of craving? he wondered, dizzily. When had the thought—the mere *thought*—of a kiss made his blood race and his body throb? He couldn't answer either question simply because he couldn't remember feeling this aroused in his entire life.

'Your son—did he drop out of school because he was ill?' Eleanor repeated, setting down the glass with a tiny clatter that made him jump.

'No.' Daniel took a deep breath as bile rose to his throat, the bitter taste of guilt and betrayal. How could he have imagined that what he had felt just now had been more potent than what he had felt for Camille? It was hard to hide his dismay as he continued. 'His mother died and it sent Nathan off the rails for a while. Thankfully, he got himself together in the end but it was a struggle. That's why he's my number one priority and always will be. I owe it to Camille to make sure our son has a happy and fulfilling life.'

CHAPTER SIX

ELLIE DIDN'T KNOW what to say. She had deliberately avoided delving into Daniel's personal life. It had seemed the sensible thing to do, to maintain her distance. However, finding out that his wife had died was a shock, even more so when she could tell by his expression that he was still grieving. Picking up the glass, she took another sip of wine while she searched for something to say but everything seemed trite. How did you offer comfort for such a huge loss?

'I'm sorry,' she finally managed.

Daniel inclined his head. 'Thank you.'

'I had no idea about your son. Or your wife.' All of a sudden Ellie felt that she should apologise for inadvertently upsetting him. 'I would never have asked you about Nathan if I'd known…' She tailed off, afraid of compounding her errors.

'It's fine. Really.'

He smiled but there was a bleakness in his eyes that told her it *did* matter, it mattered a lot. Ellie bit her lip but the words wouldn't come. Not the right ones, anyway, the ones that might make him feel better.

'It's OK, Eleanor. Honestly.' Leaning forward, he touched her hand. 'It's four years since Camille died. I'm past the stage of bursting into tears if her name is mentioned.'

'It must be hard, though,' Ellie said quietly.

'It is. But you learn to accept what's happened after a time, and that helps.' He gave her fingers a gentle squeeze then let her go. 'Having Nathan has helped as well. I've had to focus on him, especially in the beginning. It hit him extremely hard.'

'He's all right now, though?' she queried. Funnily enough, she realised that she wanted to know everything now, every little detail that she hadn't wanted to hear before, although she wasn't sure why.

'Oh, yes. He's got his act together and is planning to go to university next year if he gets the grades. And that is something I never thought would happen a couple of years ago.'

'Good. I'm glad everything has worked out,' she said truthfully.

'Thank you. But how about you? Are you over whatever caused you to move up here?'

'How did you know?' she began, then stopped when she realised how revealing it was.

'That something bad had happened to you?' He sighed. 'Most people don't abandon a promising career and move hundreds of miles away from everything they know unless they're trying to escape from a very painful situation, Eleanor. It doesn't take a genius to work it out, does it?'

'I suppose not,' she conceded.

'So, do you want to talk about it?' He smiled at her, his eyes filled with warmth. 'I'm a good listener, I promise you.'

'There's not a lot to talk about.' She shrugged, not sure if she wanted to disclose all the unsavoury details. Would it help or would it make her feel even worse if Daniel knew how she had been humiliated? It was hard to decide yet in the end the words came tumbling out, almost as though she needed to rid herself of them. 'It's an all too familiar story, I'm afraid. I was engaged to be married until I discovered that my fiancé was sleeping with someone else.'

'It must have been a shock even if you aren't the first woman it's happened to,' Daniel said gently.

'It was, although I should have realised that something was going on.' She gave a bitter laugh. 'The signs were all there. I just failed to read them properly!'

Daniel frowned. 'What do you mean?'

'That Michael—my ex—had been behaving strangely for months, cancelling dates or claiming that he was meeting friends for a drink. I just accepted what he said without questioning it, more fool me!'

'It's easy to be wise after the event,' he said quietly. 'But you were engaged so it was only natural that you believed him.'

'That's what my parents said.' Ellie sighed. 'I felt such a fool, though, especially when Gemma said that it had been clear to everyone that Michael had been leading me on.'

'Not the kindest thing to have said,' Daniel observed, frowning. 'Who's Gemma?'

'My sister. Or, to be absolutely correct, my adopted sister, although that isn't right either as I'm the one who was adopted.' Ellie realised that she wasn't making much sense but talking about what had happened wasn't easy. She took a deep breath, forcing herself to speak calmly and rationally. Daniel didn't need her gibbering on like an emotional wreck.

'I was adopted as a baby, you see. Apparently, my parents had given up any hope of having a child of their own so they decided to adopt. Then, eight years later, Mum discovered she was pregnant and along came Gemma.'

'I see. And how did you two get on? Were you close?'

'Not really. We were very different even as children. I was rather shy and introverted, whereas Gemma was far more outgoing. Oh, my parents did their best not to show any favouritism but they couldn't help it. Gemma was the child they had longed for and they adored her.'

'Did you resent it, that they appeared to love her more than you?' Daniel said softly.

'I'm not sure resent is the right word,' Ellie said, slowly. Funnily enough, she had never tried to work out how she felt about the family dynamics before. 'I suppose I just accepted that was how things were. My parents loved me, and I knew it, but they loved Gemma more. The only thing I can remember thinking was that I had to be better behaved than Gemma.'

'You felt that you had to earn their love?' Daniel observed, and she frowned.

'I suppose so.' She looked up and felt her heart lurch when she saw the way he was looking at her with such concern. Daniel cared about what she was telling him. He cared about *her*. The thought unlocked the last of her reservations. 'Gemma and I didn't see very much of each other once I went to university—she had her life and I had mine. I introduced Michael to her when I took him home to meet my family and they seemed to get along well enough. I had no idea she had reservations about him.'

'Where did you meet him?'

'At work. He was a junior partner, the same as me.' She shrugged. 'To be honest, I didn't take to him at first. He had very strong views and could be, well, rather bombastic at times. Then the head of the practice invited us both to dinner one night and things progressed from there.'

She paused, needing a moment before she told Daniel the rest. 'Anyway, we started seeing one another and eventually became engaged. Michael used to joke that it would be good for his career as the senior partners were very keen on folk being married rather than merely living together. They thought it lent stability to the practice.'

'Hmm. I see,' Daniel said dryly, and she sighed.

'You're wondering if that was the reason he was so keen to get engaged, aren't you?' She didn't wait for him to answer. 'I've wondered that myself so I don't blame you, although it's not very flattering to think that there was an ulterior motive behind it all.'

'What happened to cause you to break up?' he asked quietly.

'I found him in bed with one of the practice nurses. It was a Saturday morning. Michael had told me that he was going out for a drink with a couple of friends from university on the Friday night so I decided to surprise him—take him some coffee in case he had overindulged and generally minister to him. I had a key to his flat so I let myself in and headed upstairs.' Ellie felt tears start to stream down her face as she recalled the moment when her life had fallen apart. 'They were in his bedroom. The door was open and as I went up the stairs, I could see him and Stacey in bed. It didn't take a genius to work out that they'd spent the night together!'

Daniel acted instinctively. Standing up, he went over to her and drew her up into his arms. He couldn't begin to describe how horrified he felt by what he had heard. That anyone could treat her that way was beyond his comprehension. All he could do was try to comfort her any way he could.

Tilting her face, he wiped away her tears with his fingers, murmuring to her under his breath.

'It's all right. I know it must hurt like crazy right now, but it will get easier, believe me.'

'Will it?' She looked at him and his heart ached when he saw the plea in her dove-grey eyes. She was desperate for reassurance and somehow he had to find a way to convince her that she would get past this low point in her life.

'Yes. No matter how painful it is at the moment, it will get better.' A single tear dripped off her lashes and he wiped it away with his fingertips. Her skin felt so soft, as soft and as smooth as satin, and a jolt of awareness flashed through him. He knew that he was stepping into dangerous territory, yet it was impossible to relinquish his hold on her when she needed to be held so much. 'You just need time, Eleanor, that's all. Time to put it all behind you. Then, when you meet someone else, it will no longer matter.'

She was shaking her head before he had finished speaking. 'I don't want to meet anyone else.

I've no intention of putting myself in the same position again.'

'You'll change your mind,' he demurred. 'Once you've had a chance to put this into perspective, it will be a very different story.'

'I doubt it!' Her eyes blazed up at him. 'I know exactly what I intend to do with my life and it doesn't involve being at the beck and call of any man. From now on I intend to answer to one person only: me!'

She stepped back, effectively breaking his hold on her. Daniel felt a wave of sadness wash over him. Eleanor was turning her back on love. She planned to live her life on her own, never marry and probably never have a family either. He couldn't bear to imagine her leading such a lonely existence.

'Eleanor,' he began, then stopped when his phone rang. Taking it out of his pocket, he felt his stomach sink when he discovered it was Nathan calling. Basketball practice wasn't due to finish for another half-hour and he couldn't help worrying what was wrong. 'Is everything all right?'

he demanded, turning away while he answered the call. He felt his anxiety subside as Nathan explained why he was phoning. 'OK, I'll be there as soon as I can.'

He ended the call and turned to Eleanor. 'That was Nathan. They've finished early because the lights in the gym have fused. I'll have to go and fetch him.'

'Of course.'

She led the way from the room and Daniel could tell that she was making an effort to collect herself. That she regretted her outburst was obvious and he sighed. Eleanor had grown used to hiding her feelings while she had been growing up but he wasn't convinced it was a good thing. Sometimes it did more harm than good to bottle things up, although he doubted if she would appreciate him telling her that. He was trying to rid himself of the thought of how lonely she was going to be if she carried out her plan when she turned to him.

'What about the keys?'

'Oh. Yes, of course.' Daniel took them out of his pocket, silently berating himself for forgetting the reason why he had come. He'd got so caught up in Eleanor's affairs that it had slipped his mind. 'It's quite straightforward,' he said hurriedly. 'The Yale key unlocks the front door and the other one is for the back. The alarm cupboard is behind the reception desk and the code is 7826. You just need to key it in and that'll stop the alarm going off.'

Daniel busied himself with practicalities, relieved to have something else to focus on. He'd had his doubts about her moving abroad and, after what she had told him, he was less convinced than ever that it was a good idea. However, it wasn't his place to tell her that. At the end of the day, it wasn't as though he could offer her an alternative, not just a job but a life that wouldn't mean her being on her own. He must never forget that Nathan came first.

The thought was strangely disquieting and he hurried on. 'Would you like me to write it down for you?'

'There's no need,' she said quietly. '7826—I'll remember it.'

'Excellent!' Daniel winced when heard the

falsely hearty note in his voice but there was nothing he could do about it. Eleanor had opened the door and it was clear that she expected him to leave now that he had done what he had come for.

Zipping up his coat, he went to step past her, pausing when she said quietly, 'Drive carefully. The wind's really strong tonight.'

'I will.' He wasn't sure what prompted him to do what he did next. Maybe it was her unexpected show of concern but he bent and kissed her on the cheek. His lips lingered for the briefest of moments before he drew back, but he could feel the impact of what he had done spreading throughout his entire body. 'Goodnight, Eleanor,' he said, his voice sounding so strained that it was like hearing a stranger's voice, but in a way that was what he was, a stranger to himself, a person he no longer recognised.

'Goodnight.'

Her voice drifted after him as he ran down the steps. It seemed to follow him as he made his way round to the car park. Daniel got into his car then sat staring through the windscreen. After Camille had died, he had felt numb. The long months they had spent fighting the cancer that had eventually claimed her had left him drained. There had been nothing left inside him, not even anger at the fact that he had lost the woman he had loved. The only emotion he'd felt had been the need to protect Nathan. Oh, he had cared about his patients and had wanted to do his best for them, but, personally, he had felt nothing. Wanted nothing. Needed nothing. But not any longer.

Daniel drove out of the car park, forcing himself to concentrate as he drove along the narrow winding roads. He couldn't afford to let his mind wander, mustn't allow himself to think about what *he* wanted now. In a few months' time Eleanor would leave Beesdale, leave *him*, and go heaven knew where. That was all he needed to know.

Ellie was already in her room when Daniel arrived at the surgery the following morning. She had spent a restless night, going over what had happened, but she still wasn't sure why he had kissed her. Had it been a token gesture, like those meaningless kisses everyone exchanged on meeting or parting nowadays? Or had it been an attempt to comfort her after what she had told him? She could make a case for either and yet Daniel didn't strike her as a man who went in for kissing women in an ad hoc fashion. On the contrary, he was the kind of man who only kissed a woman when he meant it.

A frisson ran through her and she jumped up. Going over to the cupboard, she checked the shelves to make sure that she had everything she needed. She mustn't make the mistake of thinking that Daniel had kissed her because he had wanted to kiss *her*. As she knew to her cost, men were experts at disguising the truth!

'Good morning. Looks as though it's going to be another busy day. We already have a queue out there.'

Ellie swung round when she heard Daniel's voice. He was standing in the doorway and there was something about the way he was looking at her, a kind of wariness to his expression that made her heart surge. Had he been thinking about that kiss as well? Thinking about it and remembering how it had felt? For if she had spent time trying to work out why it had happened, she had spent an equal amount of time recalling how his lips had felt when they had touched her cheek…

A shudder ran through her and she gripped hold of the shelf when she felt her legs start to tremble. The memory of how warm his lips had felt as they had brushed her cheek had imprinted itself into her mind and it would take a long time before she rid herself of the memory. 'Ahem…yes. It looks like it,' she murmured, struggling to get a grip.

'Well, I'd better make a start. I don't want to create a backlog so early in the day.'

He gave her a quick smile then left and she heard his footsteps echoing along the corridor. Ellie went and sat down at her desk, refusing to let herself think any more about that kiss or its whys and wherefores. It had happened. Period. Pressing the button, she summoned her first patient, determined to put the incident behind her. However, in her heart she knew it wouldn't be possible to do that. That kiss had changed things, changed her, even though she wasn't sure how.

Her first patient was Nigel Walsh. A good-looking man in his forties, he cut an imposing figure, somewhat belied by the anxiety on his face as he sat down. 'So what can I do for you today, Mr Walsh?' Ellie asked, smiling at him. It was surprising how nervous even the most confident of people could become when they needed to consult a doctor and she wanted to put him at his ease.

'I've not come about me.' Nigel Walsh leant forward, looking even more strained. 'It's my wife, Madeleine. I'm extremely worried about her and that's why I've come to see you.'

'I'm afraid I can't discuss another patient with you, not even if it's your wife,' Ellie explained gently.

'What if I tell you that I'm afraid she's going to really harm herself?' Nigel Walsh ran his hand through his perfectly groomed hair. 'I'm at my wits' end, Doctor. I have no idea what to do or how to help her.'

Ellie frowned. This definitely wasn't what she

had expected to hear. 'Why do you think she may harm herself?'

'Because her behaviour is getting worse. At first it was just cutting herself, but in the last few months it's been spiralling out of control. She threw herself down the stairs last week and then, yesterday, I found her in the kitchen, holding her arm over the gas ring...' He broke off and gulped. 'I don't think I can take much more. And then there's Alice. What's it doing to her to see her mother doing all these things to herself?'

'Does your wife have a history of self-harm?' Eleanor asked, feeling in a real quandary. Patient confidentiality meant that she shouldn't discuss Mrs Walsh's behaviour even with her husband; however, if what he said was true, it appeared the woman urgently needed help.

'Oh, yes. According to her parents it started when she was a teenager but she had counselling and she was all right after that. Then, after we had Alice, it started up again, just little things at first—cuts and bruises—clumsiness, Madeleine claimed. However, it's gone way beyond that now and I've no idea what to do for the best.'

'Have you tried to get her to see someone?' Ellie asked.

'Of course I have!' Walsh sounded angry now. 'I made an appointment for her to see a psychotherapist but she refused to go. That's why I've come today, to see if you can talk some sense into her.'

'I can certainly ask her to come in and see me,' Ellie said carefully. 'But if what you say is true, she really needs specialist help.'

'Of course it's true!' the man exploded. 'Why would I make up something like this? Oh, I get it. You think I've been abusing her and that's why she keeps turning up with all those injuries.' He leapt to his feet. 'Well, I am not a wife-beater, Doctor. Far from it!'

He stormed out of the room before Ellie could stop him. Jumping up, she ran after him but he had already left. She went back to her room, wondering what she should do. She couldn't leave it like this, not when there was the risk of Mrs Walsh doing herself serious harm. No, she would have to speak to Daniel and see what he thought was the best course of action. Her heart lurched at the thought of them working together to resolve this issue. Even though she knew it was foolish, she couldn't deny that the idea appealed...

Ellie sighed as she pressed the buzzer to summon her next patient. She had to stop thinking like that. Maybe she did like Daniel but it wouldn't progress beyond liking. She had made her plans for the future and love and all the rest of it didn't feature in them.

CHAPTER SEVEN

ELLIE WAS SURPRISED to find Daniel in the office when she went to file some requests for hospital appointments. It was gone six and the rest of the staff had left. He glanced round and she couldn't help noticing how tired he looked.

'I didn't know you were still here.'

'Snap.' She shrugged when he looked blankly at her, regretting her flippancy. She had decided that the best way to handle this situation was by maintaining a strictly professional demeanour whenever she was with him and remarks like that wouldn't help. Last night she had overstepped the boundaries by telling him about Michael and she needed to redress the balance. 'Actually, I'm glad you're still here,' she said more formally. 'I wanted to speak to you about something that happened this morning.'

'Oh, and what was that?' he asked, turning to face her. Ellie felt her heart give another of those unsettling little lurches as she suddenly found herself the subject of his attention. It was an effort to concentrate on what she wanted to say.

'I had a man come to see me this morning, not about himself but about his wife. Apparently, she's been self-harming and her behaviour is spiralling out of control.'

'Really?' Daniel frowned. 'I take it that she's a patient here?'

'Yes. Madeleine Walsh—do you know her?'

'I do. In fact, she came in only last week because she'd hurt her arm falling down the stairs. Turned out that it was just badly sprained but it could easily have been broken.' His expression darkened. 'I take it her husband is claiming that she did it to herself?'

'Yes. That's right. Why? Do you think he was lying?' Ellie asked, in surprise.

'I think it's possible. Walsh wouldn't be the first to lay the blame for his actions on his victim. It's an old trick, I hate to tell you.'

Ellie bridled when she heard what sounded very much like condescension in his voice. That Daniel believed she was too gullible to recognise the excuses some people used to cover up their behaviour stung. Michael had displayed the same high-handed attitude towards her at times, but she was nobody's fool and it was time Daniel understood that.

'I am well aware of that,' she said curtly. 'However, I don't believe that was what Mr Walsh was trying to do. He's genuinely worried about his wife, in my opinion, and I feel that I should take his concerns seriously. It's not just Mrs Walsh I need to think about, after all. They have a young child and I intend to ensure that she isn't put at risk. However, I apologise for involving you. I'll sort this out myself.'

Ellie spun round, refusing to stand there and beg Daniel to believe her. He would accept that she was right or he wouldn't, but it was up to him. No matter what he thought, she intended to do something about this situation.

'Wait!'

She stopped reluctantly when Daniel called her back, hating the fact that she felt so upset. Why should it matter if he thought she was wrong? It didn't make sense, or not the kind of sense she was willing to accept. Admitting that she cared what he thought about her was too dangerous; it hinted at a closeness she didn't want to foster. She'd had her chance at the happy-ever-after and it had failed. Miserably. She'd be a fool to dip her toes into that particular water again!

Daniel could have bitten off his tongue. It was obvious that he had upset Eleanor and that was the last thing he wanted to do. Nevertheless, he knew it would be wrong to let her carry on believing Walsh's claims when the man was undoubtedly playing her for a fool. The thought cranked up his anger another notch so that his tone was gruffer than it otherwise might have been.

'Why do you believe that Walsh was telling you the truth?' he said brusquely.

'It's obvious that you've made up your mind about him so I can't see any point in discussing it,' she shot back.

'Maybe not, but indulge me.' He stared at her, watching the angry colour flood her cheeks. Despite the fact that she gave off that aura of coolness, there was passion bubbling beneath the surface. The thought sent a flash of heat through him and he cleared his throat, afraid that he would give himself away. Knowing that Eleanor felt such passion was strangely erotic.

'I've never met Walsh so I'm basing my opinion on what Madeleine Walsh told me,' he said flatly, determined to get a grip on his emotions. He held up his hand when she went to interrupt. 'Just hear me out, will you? She seemed frightened when I suggested contacting her husband so he could drive her to hospital to have her wrist X-rayed. She was also deliberately vague at first about how she came to fall down the stairs. Then, when I pressed her, she went into all kinds of detail about how it had happened.'

'All classic signs of someone suffering abuse.' Eleanor sighed. 'There were a couple of cases where I worked before, a man and a woman who were being abused by their partners. It was hard to get them to admit what was happening so I could set things in motion and try to help them.'

'Exactly,' Daniel agreed, regretting his earlier comments more than ever. It appeared that Eleanor had experience of this type of situation so maybe he should listen to what she was saying and not jump to conclusions.

The thought that he was guilty of that hit him hard, especially coming on top of the guilt he already felt about what had happened the night before. Maybe that kiss had been no more than a token but it had aroused a lot of emotions inside him, guilt being the biggest one of all. How could he have kissed Eleanor like that? How could he have forgotten, even for a moment, about Camille? She had never even entered his head and he knew that the fact he had forgotten about her would continue to upset him.

'The situation is very similar with people who self-harm, though, isn't it? They go to great lengths to hide what they're doing too.' Eleanor's voice roused him and he nodded, relieved to think about something else.

'Yes, that's true. They're ashamed of their actions, even though they feel compelled to continue hurting themselves.'

'Then can't you see that Madeleine Walsh could fall into that category…that she's self-harming rather than being abused?'

'I'll admit you could be right, although I'm still not convinced. Apparently, Nigel Walsh is a solicitor, a very good one from all accounts too. He must be adept at presenting his case,' Daniel observed, flatly, reluctant to concede that she was right. Maybe he was holding out as a kind of defence mechanism, refuting Eleanor's claims because he didn't want to side with her. He sighed, knowing he was wrong to allow his personal feelings to skew his judgement this way.

'Look, Eleanor—' he began, then stopped when the phone suddenly rang.

Lifting it off its rest, he listened intently to what the caller was saying. 'Right. I'll meet you there…' He stopped and listened again then glanced at Eleanor. 'I'll sort something out. Leave it with me.'

'Has something happened?'

Daniel turned when Eleanor spoke, doing his best to find a level. Maybe that kiss had knocked him for six but he had to put it into perspective. It had been just one moment out of his life, one tiny episode that would soon be forgotten if he didn't keep thinking about it. He had to let it go and not keep on poking at it like an aching tooth.

'There's been an incident,' he said, deliberately confining his thoughts to the present.

'An incident?' Ellie repeated, confused by the swift change of subject. One minute they had been discussing the Walshes and the next—this.

'Yes. A party of teenagers doing their Duke of Edinburgh Award left the hostel where they're staying just before eight this morning and they haven't been seen since.' Daniel sounded worried, as well he might, Ellie realised, glancing at her watch. Twelve hours was a long time for the youngsters to be out on the hills. She had no difficulty focusing on what he was saying as he continued.

'The staff who've accompanied them have checked the route they should have taken and they're nowhere to be found. We can only conclude that they've got themselves lost, which is why the mountain rescue team has been called in. I'm part of the team so I'll be going along but we need another doctor. Is there any chance that you'd come along, Eleanor?'

Daniel watched as one of the rescue team spread an Ordnance Survey map across the bonnet of the vehicle and weighted it down with stones. The wind was howling across the hills now, heralding the arrival of the storm that had been forecast that night. Quite frankly, the teenagers couldn't have chosen a worse time to have gone missing. He glanced at Eleanor and could tell that she was thinking the same as him. For some reason the thought sent a little thrill of pleasure coursing through him.

'Right, guys, gather round.' Joe Thorne, leader of the local cave and mountain rescue team, called them to order. Daniel hurriedly cleared his head of any more such foolish ideas as Joe pointed to a red line that had been marked on the map. He needed to focus rather than allow his mind to run off at tangents.

'That's the route the kids were supposed to take,' Joe explained. 'We know they followed it for several miles as one of their teachers found a water bottle belonging to the group. However, it appears that they wandered off course, probably around here.'

Daniel frowned when Joe pointed to the Witch's Cauldron, so-called because the deep depression in the land was shaped like a gigantic bowl. Although the view from the surrounding cliffs might be spectacular, it was also one of the most dangerous places around. Rock falls were rife and many a walker had been caught out when the ground had given way beneath him.

'It's not going to be easy to get there let alone find them in this storm but we can't wait until the morning,' Joe continued. 'Although the teachers are adamant that the group are properly kitted out, I doubt if any of the kids has experience of being outside in weather like this. We need to find them and find them fast.'

There was a murmur of agreement from the team. Daniel knew they were all aware how quickly hypothermia could set in under these conditions. He turned to Eleanor, wanting to make sure that she understood the dangers too. 'Hypothermia is going to be our biggest problem, for us as well as for those kids. Your body temperature can drop before you're aware of it.'

'I understand.' Eleanor pulled the collar of the waterproof jacket around her neck. She didn't possess any waterproofs so Daniel had called at his house and collected an old set of Nathan's. The trousers were far too long for her but she had rolled them up and used string to tie them around her ankles. A pair of Nathan's outgrown walking boots, worn with several pairs of socks, had solved the problem of her footwear too. Daniel was as sure as he could be that she was suitably protected against the elements but he still intended to keep a watch over her. The last thing he wanted was her coming to any harm.

The thought made his stomach churn and he turned away, not wanting her to suspect how worried he felt. Not for the first time that night he found himself cursing Bernard Hargreaves for refusing to come along. He didn't believe the other man's claim that he wasn't feeling well. Bernard had been doing the bare minimum for months now and Daniel knew that he would have to do something about it. He had let it slide because he'd had too much else to think about, what with Nathan and his exams, and Beth going on maternity leave. Nevertheless, there was no way that the situation could continue indefinitely. No way he would let it!

Once again, Daniel was surprised by the strength of his reaction. He hadn't realised how flat he had felt for the last few years. His concern for Nathan had used up every scrap of energy he'd possessed and there had been nothing left for anything else. Now, all of a sudden, he felt different, more alive, more in touch with his feelings. It was as though he had surfaced from some dark place and stepped back into the light. Was it a good thing? He wasn't sure. In that dark place he'd not had to think about himself, about his needs and his desires; he'd only had to exist.

It was an unsettling thought so it was a relief when Joe started to divide the group into teams. They could cover more ground if they split up, although Daniel wasn't happy at the idea of Eleanor being sent off with someone else. She had no experience of this kind of terrain and he would never forgive himself if she got hurt when he was responsible for her being there. He drew Joe aside, wanting to make the position clear.

'I'm not happy about Eleanor wandering around in this storm,' he said bluntly, not wasting any time. The sooner they found the missing teenagers the better and there was no point beating around the bush. 'I'd prefer it if she stayed here at base.'

'I understand your concerns but surely the whole point of her coming along was to act as back-up if more than one of the group is injured,' Joe pointed out. 'OK, we're all trained in first aid, but with Alan in hospital we don't have the medical know-how to deal with any serious injuries.'

Daniel knew he was right. Alan Hunter, a former paramedic and mainstay of the team, had suffered a heart attack a couple of weeks earlier and they hadn't found a replacement for him yet. It was the reason why Daniel had asked Eleanor to come along after Bernard had refused, and he could hardly go back on his decision. He sighed. 'All right, but can you keep an eye on her? She's no experience and I don't want her coming to any harm.'

'Don't you worry—she'll be perfectly safe. We're going to stick to the main path so it shouldn't be too difficult for her to keep up.'

Joe didn't say anything else but Daniel saw the look the other man gave him and felt himself colour. He turned away, refusing to speculate about what Joe was thinking. He would be equally concerned about anyone who had so little experience, he assured himself as he swung his backpack over his shoulder. However, even to his ears the claim had a hollow ring. He was concerned because it was Eleanor and, like it or not, she was special.

Eleanor trudged on, bracing herself against the wind. The storm was raging around them now, the rain forming horizontal sheets as it pelted across

the hillside. She had never been out in weather
like this before and she found it exhilarating to
test herself against the elements. If she could survive this, she could survive anything!

'All right?'

She looked round when Joe Thorne came along-
side her. 'Yes, although this wind is something
else. I've never been out in a gale like this before.'

'Welcome to the Dales,' Joe replied, tongue very
firmly tucked in his cheek. 'The weather here
takes some getting used to but you're doing great.'
He laughed. 'At least I don't need to worry about
falling foul of the doc now. I got the impression
he'd have my guts for garters if anything happened to you!'

He moved away, leaving Ellie to digest what he
had said. Daniel had been worried about her—really? The thought sent a rush of warmth through
her even though she knew how stupid it was. They
trudged on for another mile or so. Ellie's legs were
starting to ache now, unused to having to carry
her over such rough terrain. When Joe called a
halt she sank down onto a rock and rubbed her

aching calves, determined that she was going to keep up with the others. The last thing she wanted was to be a burden to them, she thought, then glanced round when she heard what sounded like a shout coming from behind her. The rest of the team were gathered around Joe, checking the map, and didn't appear to have heard anything, and she frowned. Had she imagined it?

Ellie sat quite still, listening. The wind was howling now and it was difficult to hear anything above the noise it was making. She had just decided that it had been her imagination when she heard it again. Jumping up, she ran over to Joe. 'I heard a shout!' She pointed towards the rock she'd been sitting on. 'It seemed to come from over there.'

'Right, let's take a look.' Joe led the way, the others fanning out on either side of him. Ellie wasn't as quick as they were but she did her best to keep up. She gasped when she spotted a figure lying on the ground. Hurrying forward, she dropped to her knees beside the girl. She was soaking wet and shivering violently. It was obvious that she was in the first stages of hypothermia and Ellie knew that she urgently needed to warm her up.

'My name's Ellie and I'm a doctor,' she told her. 'What's your name?'

'Hannah.' The girl could hardly speak because her teeth were chattering.

'Right, Hannah, can you tell me if you've hurt yourself?'

'My ankle—I think I've broken it,' Hannah managed.

Ellie took a look at her right ankle while one of the team shone a torch onto it. She sighed when she saw how swollen it was. 'Hmm, it looks very painful. I won't try to remove your boot. We'll leave that until we get you to hospital as it will be less painful to do it there. Is there anything else—cuts, bruises, anything at all?'

'No, just my ankle. That's why I couldn't go back to find the others.' Hannah bit her lip as tears started to pour down her cheeks. 'I should never have gone off and left them then this wouldn't have happened!'

'Let's worry about that later,' Ellie said firmly. 'We need to get you warm at the moment.' Unzipping the girl's sodden jacket, she slid it off. Hannah was wearing a T-shirt underneath and it too was soaking wet.

'Get that off her as well, Doc,' Joe instructed, taking a thermal top from his backpack. He helped Ellie get it on the girl then added a fleece jacket over the top with a foil blanket over that. Within a remarkably short time, Hannah was being strapped to a stretcher. Ellie also helped to fit an inflatable splint around the girl's ankle to prevent it being jolted on the way to the rescue vehicle. Taking out his radio, Joe contacted the rest of the team to let them know what was happening and they set off.

Ellie could feel her legs trembling as she struggled to keep her footing on the rain-slick path. How the men carrying the stretcher managed to remain upright was beyond her. By the time they reached the vehicles she was exhausted but she had to find the reserves to keep going somehow. Until Hannah had been handed over to the team at the hospital, she was her responsibility. It took the best part of an hour to reach the hospital. Ellie kept a close watch on Hannah, knowing that she wasn't out of danger yet. Hypothermia could still set in and that was the last thing they wanted. It was a relief to finally hand her over to the A and E staff, who rushed her off to Resus. At least, the girl would receive the care she needed now.

'They've found the rest of the kids.' Joe came back into the waiting area after having gone outside to answer his phone. He grinned at Ellie and the others. 'They were sheltering in a cave close to the Witch's Cauldron. They're cold and wet but otherwise unharmed.'

'Thank heaven for that!' Ellie exclaimed. 'Have they said what happened?'

'Apparently, Hannah and another girl had an argument over one of the boys. It seems he's been playing the field and, when Hannah found out, she went storming off. When she didn't come back, the others tried to find her and got themselves lost.' Joe rolled his eyes. 'The course of true love has a lot to answer for!'

Everyone laughed, including Ellie, although she couldn't help thinking how true the comment was. Love could ruin a person's life, as she knew to her cost. It made her see that any thoughts she may have been harbouring about trying again in the future had been madness. Why expose herself to the risk of heartache all over again?

'Oh, by the way, Ellie, I told the doc that we'd drop you off at home. There didn't seem any point in him driving over here to collect you,' Joe told her as they left the hospital. 'I hope that was OK?'

'Of course.' Ellie dredged up a smile, not wanting Joe to suspect that she felt the tiniest bit disappointed. She took a quick breath, knowing how stupid it was. She had just decided that she was going to stick to her decision to focus on her career so what was the point of wishing she could have spent more time with Daniel? 'Thanks, Joe. I appreciate it.'

'No problem,' Joe said cheerfully, unlocking the car. They all piled in, squeezing into whatever space they could find. Ellie found herself tucked into a gap between the various piles of equipment.

It wasn't the most comfortable of position but it was better than waiting around for Daniel, she assured herself. Just for a moment the image of his handsome face floated before her eyes before she blanked it out. She knew what she had to do and she wasn't going to change her mind. For anyone.

CHAPTER EIGHT

THE DAY OF Sandra and Tim's barbecue dawned bright and clear. After the recent rain, it was a relief to enjoy some dry weather for once. Everyone from the surgery had been invited and were looking forward to it. Sandra and Tim were excellent hosts and their barbecues were renowned as fun occasions. Daniel, however, had mixed feelings about the evening. Whilst it would be good to socialise with his friends and colleagues, he was wary of doing or saying the wrong thing around Eleanor.

There had been a marked chill about the way she had treated him since the night they had gone looking for the missing teenagers. Although she was unfailingly polite, she had made it clear that she preferred to keep her distance. He had no idea what he had done but it was obvious that he had upset her. The thought of spending the evening tiptoeing around her wasn't appealing, especially when he knew that if it had been anyone else he would have asked them what the matter was. However, for some reason he was wary of doing that with Eleanor. And his own ambivalence unsettled him even more.

Although it was a busy day, they finished on time for once. Daniel had offered to lock up so that Marie and the rest of the staff could rush off home to get changed. He set the alarm then headed to his car. Nathan had been invited as well as he was friendly with Sandra and Tim's son, Jack. It wasn't often that Daniel got the chance to spend an evening with his son; between his college work and various sporting activities, Nathan was usually busy of an evening.

At any other time, Daniel knew that he would be looking forward to them having some time together, but Eleanor's attitude had cast a pall over the evening even though he knew it was ridiculous to let it affect him. So she didn't want to be friends with him—so what? As long as she did her job what did it matter? And yet deep down he knew that it did matter, that it mattered a great deal. He wanted to be her friend, to have her confide in him and turn to him for help, even though he couldn't understand why.

The party was in full swing by the time he and Nathan arrived. Sandra came to greet them, shaking her head. 'At last! I thought you two had got lost.'

'Sorry. My fault. I ended up sorting out some bills that I've been meaning to pay,' Daniel explained, aware that it was only partially true. Fair enough, he had ended up writing out some cheques but it had been more a delaying tactic than a necessity. His eyes skimmed over the people gathered in the garden and his heart sank when he spotted Eleanor. He had delayed leaving home because he had been reluctant to find himself on the receiving end of any more chilly treatment. How pathetic was that!

'There's Jack,' Nathan announced as Sandra excused herself to greet some more late arrivals. 'See you later, Dad.'

Daniel watched as his son headed over to where a group of youngsters had gathered. The sound of their laughter carried across to him and he sighed. Nathan seemed happy enough and now it was his turn to join the fray. Maybe he was persona non grata in Eleanor's eyes but he could hardly stand here on his own like Billy-no-mates, could he? Steeling himself, he headed over to the group from the surgery.

'Good evening, everyone,' he said, forcing himself to smile as he looked around. Marie was there with her husband, Ken, and Polly was with her fiancé, Martin. Lucy was there as well, although she was on her own as her boyfriend, James, a firefighter, was working that night. His gaze moved from one smiling face to another before it came to rest on Eleanor and he felt his heart sink even further when she nodded coolly at him. What on earth had he done to upset her?

Ellie felt her stomach churn. She had been dreading this moment when she would be forced to speak to Daniel, so much so that she had been tempted to phone Sandra and make some excuse as to why she couldn't go. However, the thought of spending the evening on her own had been an even worse prospect.

She had done her best to ignore the fact that it was her birthday, even going so far as to leave the card and present her parents had sent her unopened. She didn't need any reminders about how different this birthday was going to be compared to the last, but the downside was that she would have to socialise with Daniel and she wasn't sure if it was wise.

Oh, it had been easy enough in work; any conversations had been strictly confined to their patients. However, an occasion like this was very different. She would have to make the usual small talk and that was what worried her. The more she got to know Daniel, the more she grew to like him.

The conversation flowed on. Polly and Martin were getting married the following Easter and Lucy asked them about their plans. Marie chipped in, reminiscing about her own wedding many years earlier. Eleanor was happy to let them talk and merely listen. Although Daniel added the odd comment, he was almost as quiet as her, she noticed. She glanced at him and felt her heart leap when she met his eyes and saw the question they held. Was he wondering why she was behaving so distantly? She sensed it was true but there was no way she could explain that it was what she needed to do rather than run the risk of becoming involved with him. After all, Daniel hadn't given any sign that he was interested in her. On the contrary, he had made it clear that he was still very much in love with his late wife.

It was a depressing thought. Ellie was still trying to deal with it when Tim called for silence. 'Right, folks, I have it on good authority...' he paused and looked meaningfully at his wife before continuing '...that someone here tonight is celebrating a birthday. So I would like you all to join me in drinking a toast to Ellie. Happy birthday, love!'

Ellie flushed when everyone raised their glasses. She had forgotten that she had told Sandra it was her birthday that day and hadn't been prepared for this. Now she found her mind swooping back to the previous year before she could stop it. Michael had showered her with presents: roses and champagne at breakfast; lunch at a Michelin-starred restaurant; an evening at the Opera. Tears prickled her eyes as it struck her how very different this year was.

'Well, you certainly kept that quiet!' Marie declared, sounding put out. 'You never said a word about it being your birthday!'

'I didn't think it was worth making a fuss,' Ellie murmured, feeling guilty.

'Hmm, you still should have said something.' Stepping forward, she kissed Ellie on the cheek then wagged a finger at her. 'We'll let you off this time, so long as you bring in some cakes tomorrow. Deal?'

'Deal,' Ellie agreed, laughing. Ken kissed her as well, quickly followed by Polly and Martin, and then Lucy.

'Happy birthday, Eleanor.' Daniel stepped forward, hesitating only briefly before he bent and kissed her on the cheek. 'May the coming year bring you everything you want,' he said softly so that only she could hear.

He stepped back but it was several seconds before Ellie moved. She put her hand to her cheek, feeling her skin tingling where Daniel's lips had touched it. None of the other people's kisses had left its mark on her but Daniel's had. Why? What was so special about his kiss?

It was a relief when Tim announced the barbecue was ready. Ellie followed the others as people started to queue up. Daniel was ahead of her and her eyes lingered on the strong line of his back. He was a very attractive man so was that the reason she had reacted differently to his kiss? She could see the sense in that yet she had difficulty believing it. She had met other attractive men but not responded to them this way, had she? Why, even with Michael she hadn't felt the awareness she felt whenever she was around Daniel.

Although Michael was very good looking, she had never been overwhelmed by desire for him. In fact, she knew that Michael had grown impatient when she had refused to sleep with him at first, but she had been unwilling to compromise her views. After a couple of less than satisfying relationships, she had decided that sex needed commitment for it to mean anything. Admittedly, she had never found it that fulfilling when she and Michael had finally made love after they'd got engaged, but she had told herself it would get better with time. Now, all of a sudden, she found herself wondering if she'd been wrong, if it wasn't commitment that made a difference but the person. If she slept with Daniel, for instance, wouldn't it feel wonderful? The thought shocked her so much that she found it impossible to focus on what was happening. When Daniel turned and handed her a plate, she stared blankly at it.

'Are you all right, Eleanor?'

His deep voice rumbled softly, stirring her already heightened senses, and Ellie shivered. What would Daniel think if he knew what thoughts were going on inside her head? Would he be shocked or merely accept them as any experienced adult would do? Had she been naïve to believe that sex could only be enjoyed within certain boundaries?

Wrong to assume that it needed commitment to make it feel right? She took a deep breath, trying to contain a rush of fear as the next question flowed into her head: Was it time she found out?

Daniel had no idea what was going on but the expression on Eleanor's face worried him. Taking the plate out of her unresisting hand, he placed it back on the pile then led her from the queue. Fortunately, the others were too interested in their supper to notice what was happening as he steered her across the garden to the old wooden gazebo. 'Sit down.' He eased her down onto the seat and sat beside her. Sandra had placed tealights in jam jars around the garden and they gave out just enough light to see by. Bending forward, he stared into Eleanor's face. 'Are you feeling all right? You seem a bit, well…out of it.'

'I'm fine.' Her voice was so low that he had trouble hearing her.

'Are you sure?' Maybe it was wrong to press her but all of a sudden he needed to know what he had done to upset her. 'You've not seemed yourself for a while, I have to say.'

'Haven't I?' she murmured, avoiding his eyes.

Daniel's breath caught when he realised that she understood exactly what he meant. So it wasn't his imagination, she *had* been keeping him at arm's length, although he was no closer to knowing why. 'No. You've been very distant since the night we went looking for those teenagers,' he said quietly. 'Did I do something to upset you?'

'Of course not.' She gave a little shrug. 'I just think it's better if I focus on my job. That's all.'

'Better? In which way?' he prompted, wanting to understand what she was saying.

'Better than getting involved,' she said flatly. 'I'm only going to be here for a few months and after that I'll go somewhere else. I don't want any…complications, quite frankly.'

Daniel wasn't sure what to say. Oh, he could appreciate her logic—he didn't need any complications in his life at the moment either. He had enough on his plate. However, the thought of her cutting herself off this way was more than he could bear.

'I don't see how it would complicate matters if we were friends, Eleanor.'

'Maybe not.' She shrugged. 'However, I'd prefer it if we stick to being colleagues.'

'Doesn't that seem a little harsh?' he suggested, his heart aching at the thought of how lonely she was going to be if she continued behaving that way. 'Everyone needs friends, people they can rely on in a crisis.'

'I don't.' She stared back at him, her face set. 'I just want to be left alone to get on with my job.'

'Oh, Eleanor!' Daniel wasn't sure why it hurt so much to hear her say that but the thought of the joyless existence it would lead to was more than he could stand. Reaching out, he grasped her by the shoulders, 'I know you've been badly hurt. And I know that today of all days—your birthday—it must make it even harder, but cutting yourself off isn't the way. You have your whole life ahead of you and you need more than work to fill it!'

Pulling her to him, he hugged her, wanting to show her what she would miss. Turning her back on love was bad enough but rejecting any offers of friendship as well was just too much and he needed to make her understand that. Her body felt so tense as he held her to him, resisting his attempts to convince her, and he groaned in frustration. He had to make her see what a terrible mistake she was making!

Whether it was that thought that spurred him on, but all of a sudden Daniel found himself bending towards her. He hadn't meant it to go any further than a hug yet the moment his mouth touched hers, he was lost. Her lips were cool from the night air, cool and as unresponsive as the rest of her, and his heart ached all the harder. It was as though she had packed up all her emotions and thrown them away. The thought of how hurt she must have been to have done that brought a lump to his throat. If he could do just one thing then he wished with all his heart that he could set her free.

'I think I saw your father heading towards the gazebo, Nathan.' Sandra's voice carried clearly on the night air. Daniel jumped as he was brought back to the present with a rush. He just had time to let Eleanor go before Nathan appeared.

'Oh, sorry—I didn't mean to interrupt,' Nathan said when he saw Eleanor.

'You didn't. Eleanor and I were just discussing a few things,' Daniel said, grateful for the fact that the dim lighting hid his discomfort. He didn't dare to imagine what his son would have thought if he had found him *kissing* Eleanor. It would have seemed like the ultimate betrayal of his mother and Daniel couldn't bear to think about the effect it might have had on him. The last thing he wanted was for Nathan's world to be turned upside down at this stage.

'You two haven't met yet, have you?' he said, hurrying on. 'Eleanor this is my son, Nathan. Eleanor is covering Beth's maternity leave,' he explained for Nathan's benefit.

'Hi, there. Good to meet you.' Nathan smiled and Daniel was relieved. Obviously, Nathan didn't suspect that anything had been going on.

'You too,' she murmured politely.

Daniel felt the tiny hairs on the back of his neck

stand to attention when he heard the quaver in her voice. Was she shocked by what had happened? he wondered. And yet it wasn't shock he could hear in her voice but something else, an emotion that eluded him… It was an effort to drag his thoughts together when he realised that Nathan was saying something. 'Sorry, what was that?'

'Jack and the rest of the guys are going into town,' Nathan repeated. 'There's a band playing at the Fox and Goose so we thought we'd check it out. Jack says I can stay here tonight so you don't need to wait for us to get back.'

'Fine. Just be careful what you're doing,' Daniel said, trying to clamp down on a familiar rush of alarm. Nathan had come a long way since the days when he had got himself into trouble, he reminded himself, and *he* had to trust him.

'Will do.' Nathan sketched them a wave then headed back to his friends. A couple of minutes later they departed.

Eleanor suddenly stood up. 'I think I'll go and sample the barbecue,' she said, avoiding his eyes.

'Good idea.'

Daniel stood up as well, at a loss to know what to do. Should he apologise for kissing her or should he ignore what had happened? The kiss had caught him unawares because he hadn't planned on it happening... Had he?

Heat fizzed along his veins as he realised with mind-boggling honesty that he had thought about kissing Eleanor more than once in the past few weeks. Oh, he hadn't planned it, per se. There had been no set time or date when it would happen, but the idea had started to set down roots. Kissing her on the cheek when he had visited her at the flat and then again tonight when he had wished her happy birthday had been mere forerunners to the main event. If Nathan hadn't appeared then he would have carried on kissing her until he had received a response, until her lips had softened, warmed, kissed him back. That was what he'd wanted, of course. He'd wanted her to respond, wanted to break down her defences and admit that she was wrong to cut herself off from everyone. Especially him.

The thought hit him with the force of a physical blow. Daniel sank back down onto the bench. There had been nothing altruistic about that kiss—it had been wholly selfish. He had kissed her because he had wanted Eleanor to respond to *him*. But what good would it do to encourage her to rely on him? What could he offer her when he had Nathan to think about? He took a deep breath but the facts had to be faced. He could end up hurting her and that was the last thing he must do.

CHAPTER NINE

ELEANOR COULDN'T SHAKE off the memory of what had happened. Oh, she tried, she tried everything she could think of, but the taste and feel of Daniel's mouth had imprinted itself into her consciousness. Finally, at four a.m. she got up and made herself a cup of tea, hoping that the age-old panacea would help her put it into perspective. It had been a kiss, a very brief one too, not something to get worked up about. And yet there was no way she could pretend that it hadn't had an effect on her, no way at all that she could simply brush it aside. Daniel had kissed her and if they hadn't been interrupted then she would have responded.

Carrying the steaming mug into the sitting room, she curled up on the sofa. That was the real nub of the problem, of course—the fact that despite everything she would have responded. She could lie to herself and pretend it wouldn't have happened but what was the point? Surprise may have held her immobile at first but she knew that she would have kissed him back and with passion too. She'd felt her desire suddenly awaken and it shocked her that she should have felt so strongly about Daniel's kiss when she had felt so little whenever Michael had kissed her. She'd thought she had loved Michael but had she? Really? Or had it been more a case of loving the *idea* of having someone special in her life?

Questions rampaged around inside her head and she closed her eyes as she tried to deal with them. Had Michael sensed that something hadn't been right with their relationship? Heaven knew, the sex hadn't been that wonderful for him as well as her, so had she been guilty of short changing him, of driving him into Stacey's arms through her own shortcomings? She didn't want to believe it but she couldn't deny it either. She had never really enjoyed sex, never experienced an overwhelming desire for intimacy. She had gone through the motions but, deep down, it had left her cold. But not tonight. Not when Daniel had kissed her. For the first time ever she had felt emotionally engaged and it scared her.

Ellie opened her eyes. She hadn't switched on any lights and, through the window, she could see the moonlight gleaming off the surrounding hills. The scene was devoid of colour, like a photographic negative. It was a bit like how she had always felt, flat and colourless, but was it how she wanted to feel for the rest of her life? Was Daniel right to insist that she should want more, that she *needed* more? Was she really content to continue living this half-existence, always feeling as though she had been relegated to the sidelines rather than being centre stage?

Her head ached as the questions pounded inside it. Ellie knew that she needed to think long and hard before she reached a decision. She needed to be absolutely sure she was doing the right thing before she made any more changes to her life. After all, she had a lot to lose. The thought of suffering another humiliation was more than she could bear but that's what she would risk if she stepped off the sidelines. Was it really worth it? She wished she knew.

A week passed, the days zipping past at a rate of knots. The weather had changed again, becoming bitterly cold. Ellie dealt with a number of patients suffering from chest infections. Some were long-term problems, borne with a kind of weary sto-icism that she came to admire. The people of the Dales were not the sort to make a fuss. Ninety-year-old Arnold Brimsdale was her final patient on the Friday morning. He came marching into the room, wheezing heavily as he sat down on the chair. A wiry old man with a full head of iron-grey hair, he fixed her with a piercing stare.

'Morning, Doctor. I've not had the pleasure of meeting you before. Marie says that you're filling in for Dr Andrews while she's off looking after her young 'un.'

'That's right.' Ellie reached across the desk and shook the old man's hand. 'Nice to meet you, Mr Brimsdale. What can I do to help today?'

'Oh, it's me chest again. This cold snap's playing havoc with me breathing.'

'I see from your notes that you have chronic bronchitis,' Ellie observed.

'Aye, that's right.' Arnold Brimsdale sighed. 'Like so many lads of my generation, I took to smoking in a big way. We had no idea the damage it could cause, you see. Folk didn't in them days. Anyway, add that to the fact that I used to work in one of the borrow pits—digging out sand and aggregates—and my lungs took a fair hammering. There was no such thing as health and safety in them days. You just got on with the job.'

'How long did you work in the pit?' Ellie asked curiously, thinking what a hard life it must have been.

'Twenty-odd years, till me dad died and I decided I'd had enough.' He shrugged. 'You didn't get a choice back then. Your dad decided where you'd work and that was it. But once he'd gone I left the pit and got a job on a farm. Best thing I ever done. All that fresh air to breathe instead of muck—' He broke off and smiled. 'Anyways,

I shan't bore you with all that, Doctor. Suffice to say that it felt as though I'd died and gone to heaven. The pity is that the years I'd spent in the pit had left their mark, although I'm better off than a lot of folk. Not so many of me pals has got to be ninety.'

'I'm sure they haven't,' Ellie agreed, admiring the old man's positive take on life. Maybe he had suffered some major setbacks but he had come through them in the end. Perhaps she could do the same?

Ellie pushed that thought to the back of her mind as she listened to Arnold's chest. It soon became apparent that he had quite a severe chest infection, something he was prone to because of his bronchitis. She filled in a script for antibiotics and emailed it to the pharmacy so that it would be ready for him to collect before he left. He used an inhaler but she could see from his notes that he had renewed his prescription the previous month so that was covered. She saw him out, holding the door open for him. There was no doubt that he was a gutsy old man and the thought that she needed to adopt a more positive approach to life reared up again.

She sighed as she went back to her desk to clear up. At some point soon she would have to make a decision about what she was going to do, either stick to her plan to focus strictly on her career or accept that she needed more than just work to fill her life, as Daniel believed. It wasn't going to be easy. There were advantages to both, as well as drawbacks, but she needed to make the right decision. She couldn't bear to think that at some point she might come to regret her actions.

Daniel had steered clear of Eleanor since the night of the barbecue. The thought that he could end up hurting her, albeit unintentionally, had made him wary of spending time around her. It wasn't difficult to keep out of her way in work; they were both so busy that it was easy enough to avoid her. Outside working hours, too, his free time was limited. Although Nathan travelled to and from college by bus, if he stayed late to take part in some sort of activity, Daniel needed to collect him. During the episode when he had run amok, Nathan had got involved in joy-riding and he had been banned from driving until he reached the age of twenty. It meant that Daniel had to ferry him here and there, but he was glad to do it, especially at the moment. It meant that he could claim, quite legitimately, that he was far too busy for a social life.

The weekend dawned, dry but cold. A field trip had been arranged for the students in Nathan's year who were studying medieval history. They were off to York before travelling on the following day to Chester. Daniel had offered to drop off both Nathan and Jack at the college so he drove them there and left them outside the gates, waiting for the coach to arrive. It was still early and the town was just preparing for the day. Saturday was market day and the stall holders were setting up.

For some reason Daniel felt reluctant to go straight back home. There was nothing urgent that needed doing and the thought of going back to an empty house held little appeal. He decided to have a coffee then buy some local produce. One of the farms made some wonderful cheeses and he fancied some with a glass of wine that evening.

The coffee shop was just opening up and he was their first customer. He ordered a double espresso and a croissant then sat down near the window. There were a few more people about now, shoppers eager to get some early bargains. Daniel watched a harassed-looking young mum pushing a pram over the cobbles. She had a toddler with her and he was intent on running off. Daniel's heart lurched when the child suddenly made a bid for freedom and ran into the road, straight into the path of a van that was backing up. Daniel shot from his seat and raced out of the café but before he could reach the child, a woman ran into the road and scooped him up. He could only see the back of her as she carried him back to his distraught mother so it wasn't until she turned round that he realised it was Eleanor.

He went to meet her as she walked back across the street, taking note of the pallor of her skin. That she'd had a shock at the near-miss was obvious. Instinctively, he placed his hand under her elbow as she came to a halt beside him. 'Are you OK?' he said solicitously, bending toward her.

'Daniel!' she exclaimed, staring at him in confusion. 'What are you doing here?'

'I was in the café when I saw what was happening. Talk about a close shave…'

'I know.' She shuddered, her face turning even paler. 'I didn't think I'd get to him in time.'

'But you did.' He smiled at her. 'Let's hope his mum puts some reins on him. He might not be so lucky next time.'

'Don't!'

She still looked deeply shaken and, despite every reservation he had, Daniel couldn't leave it there. How could he simply walk away when she'd had a shock like that? Taking a firmer grip on her arm, he steered her toward the café. 'What you need is a dose of caffeine,' he said firmly, ignoring all the warning bells that were clanging away inside him. It was what he would do for anyone, he reasoned, make sure they took time to recover before they went on their way. However, deep down he knew that the fact it was Eleanor who needed his help made a world of difference.

'Oh, but, you must have things to do.' She bit her lip and he could tell that she was doing her best not to let him see just how shaken up she felt. 'I'm fine—really I am.'

'Then why are you trembling?' He sighed when she didn't say anything. 'It's just a coffee, Eleanor, nothing more than that. I understand how you feel, believe me.'

Ellie flushed, realising how ridiculously she was behaving. Daniel was right because it had been a shock when she'd seen the child run out into the road... Another shudder passed through her. When Daniel opened the café door and ushered her inside, she didn't protest any more. He sat her down near the window then went to the counter. He came back a moment later, unwinding his scarf as he sat down.

'I've ordered you a flat white—I hope that's all right?'

'Yes, fine. Thank you.' Reaching up, she pulled off her knitted hat and placed it on the table. Normally, she never wore a hat but it was much colder here than it was down south, plus her hair was so short that she felt the chill more acutely. Running her fingers through the short black strands, she smoothed them into place as best she could.

'Here.' Reaching out, Daniel smoothed down a strand of hair that had escaped her attentions then smiled at her. 'That's better. All nice and tidy now.'

'I…erm…thank you,' Ellie muttered, feeling heat well up inside her. She hurriedly unzipped her coat and shrugged it off, hoping he would attribute her heightened colour to the layers of clothing she was wearing. No way did she want him to guess that it was his touch that had caused it.

'So what are you doing here, apart from rescuing escaping children?' he asked after the waitress had brought over their drinks.

'I thought I'd visit the market,' she explained. 'Marie said that it sells mainly local produce and I thought I'd sample what's on offer.'

'It's renowned throughout the Dales for its produce,' Daniel agreed. Picking up his cup, he took a sip of his coffee. Ellie bit her lip when she saw the sheen of moisture on his mouth as he lowered the cup. All of a sudden all she could think about was how his lips would taste if he kissed her. Would they be flavoured by the coffee, perhaps? Rich and fragrant from the aromatic beans? It was an effort to concentrate as he continued.

'The cheese stall is exceptionally good. They sell a wide range of cheeses made by local farmers and they'd give anything produced on the Continent a run for their money.' He laughed as he kissed his fingertips. 'One of their blue cheeses in particular is *magnifique*!'

Despite herself, Ellie found herself laughing. 'Obviously you're something of a connoisseur. You'll have to write down the name of it for me. My cheese buying has been confined to whatever the supermarket has in stock up till now.'

Daniel rolled his eyes. 'Your education has been sorely lacking! We'll have to do something about it. How's your coffee? Not too strong, I hope?'

'No. It's fine,' Ellie assured him, although nor-

mally she would have chosen something less potent. When he picked up the plate and offered
her the croissant, she shook her head. 'No. That's
yours.'

'We'll share then.' Daniel tore the flaky pastry
apart, placing his half on a paper napkin before
setting the plate in front of her. 'Come along, eat
up. Carbs are very good for shock.'

'Not so good for the figure,' Ellie countered ruefully, biting into the buttery rich pastry.

'Not something you need to worry about,' Daniel declared, taking an appreciative bite out of his
half.

Ellie concentrated on the pastry, refusing to let
the compliment affect her. Daniel thought she had
a good figure—so what? However, no matter how
hard she tried to dismiss the remark, it refused to
go quietly. It settled into a tiny corner of her mind
and stayed there. By the time they had finished
their coffee, several more people had come into
the café. Daniel smiled and nodded as everyone
wished him good morning. He grimaced as he
looked over at Ellie.

'The downside of being the local GP is that everyone knows you. There's no chance of being anonymous!'

'It's rather nice, though, isn't it?' Ellie said slowly. She shrugged when he looked at her in surprise. 'It must make you feel…well, a sort of *connection* to the people who live here.'

'That's true.' He glanced around the café then turned back to her. 'Being part of people's lives is a privilege, I always think. It also makes it easier when they have a problem. They already know me so there isn't that need to gain their trust—it's already there.'

'It's very different from where I worked before,' Ellie admitted. 'The population changed very rapidly as people moved in and out of the town. It was rare that we got to know our patients.'

'It makes it harder for the doctors as well as the patients, don't you think? People are reluctant to open up when they don't know you and it makes it all the more difficult to get to the root of their problems.'

'It does.' Ellie was surprised that he understood

the drawbacks. 'I didn't think you'd understand that with working here.'

'I worked at an inner city practice before I moved here,' he explained. 'Even then, the population tended to fluctuate, and it must be much worse now when people travel about to find work.'

'Is that why you came to the Dales?' she asked curiously, even though she shouldn't ask questions like that. She shouldn't be delving into Daniel's life, getting to know more about him. Even if she did decide not to cut herself off as she had planned to do, she mustn't allow herself to grow attached to him.

'Partly. Camille grew up in a very rural area of France and she never really settled in the city. I thought it would be easier for her if we moved somewhere similar. As luck would have it, a job came up here and I applied for it. It turned out to be the right thing to do. Camille loved living here. We were very happy.'

CHAPTER TEN

DANIEL HEARD THE catch in his voice and fought to control it. If he was honest, he was stunned that he felt so emotional. He had long since passed the stage of breaking down whenever Camille was mentioned so what was going on? Why was it that Eleanor seemed to possess the power to unleash his emotions this way? He had no idea but he knew that if he didn't change the subject he would regret it. Pushing back his chair, he made a determined effort to get a grip.

'Right, time to show you the delights of the market before it gets too busy,' he said with false heartiness. 'It will be bedlam here in an hour's time—we won't be able to see what's on the stalls.'

'If you're sure?' she said quietly.

Daniel felt the back of his neck prickle. Had Eleanor realised he was upset? he wondered with a sinking heart. He shot a glance at her but she was bending over to pick up her bag and he couldn't see her face… He drove the thought from his mind, determined not to make matters worse by letting it run away with him. Of course she hadn't noticed. Why should she when she didn't really know him?

'Of course I'm sure. If you don't get a guided tour then the odds are that you'll miss something.' He drummed up a smile, trying to quash the equally unsettling thought that he wished she *was* interested enough to want to get to know him. 'Let's start at the cheese stall. I guarantee that you won't be able to resist.'

Eleanor laughed as she followed him out of the café. 'You aren't on commission by any chance? Free cheese whenever you bring them a new customer?'

'What a good idea!' he exclaimed, feeling easier now that the conversation had moved on. He would steer clear of anything personal in future, he told himself as he led the way across the road. Stick to topics that wouldn't cause problems for him as well as for her. He had come to terms with Camille's death and he didn't want to start thinking about the hole it had left in his life. He should be grateful for what he'd had and not start wishing that he could experience that kind of closeness again. That would be plain greedy. One love, one lifetime. That was enough for anyone.

Wasn't it?

Ellie did her best but it was impossible to shake off the feeling of sadness. She'd heard the catch in Daniel's voice and the thought that he was still suffering was hard to bear. He must have loved his wife very much to feel this way after so much time had elapsed. Once again, she found herself thinking about Michael. She had been so sure that it had been the real thing, the kind of love that lasted for ever. However, the more she thought about it, the more doubtful she became. Could she really imagine herself still feeling so unhappy in a few years' time? It was a relief to put the thought out of her mind as they reached the cheese stall. As Daniel had promised there was a huge range of cheeses on offer. He pointed to a creamy blue cheese in the middle of the display.

'That's my favourite. It's made on a farm just a couple of miles from here and it's delicious. A chunk of that, a glass of red wine, and you're in seventh heaven.'

'High praise indeed,' Ellie declared, smiling at the young woman behind the counter. 'Have you got Dr Saunders on commission? Because I have to say that he's a wonderful advocate for your produce.'

'Not yet, but it sounds like a good idea,' the woman replied, laughing. She cut a sliver of cheese off the round and passed it to Ellie. 'See what you think.'

Ellie popped the cheese into her mouth, savouring its rich and creamy flavour. 'Mmm, it's delicious.' She glanced at Daniel, determined to keep things on an even footing. There must be no more comparing her relationship with Michael to Daniel's relationship with his late wife. It was pointless and needlessly upsetting to know that she always came off worse. 'You definitely know your cheeses, Dr Saunders.'

'What can I say?' Daniel hammed it up for all he was worth, assuming an expression of modesty. 'It's just a natural inborn talent. I can't claim any credit for it.'

'Put like that then, no, you can't.' Ellie laughed as his face fell. 'It's your own fault. You shouldn't go fishing for compliments.'

'Hm. Probably not.' He smiled ruefully at the young woman behind the counter. 'That's me put in my place, isn't it? Anyway, I'll have some of the Outhwaite Farm Wensleydale as well as that blue. I shall cheer myself up by having a cheese fest!'

They made their way round the market, stopping at the various stalls. By the time they had done a full circuit, Ellie was weighted down with bags. She shook her head in dismay. 'I only came to have a look round so I'm not sure how I ended up with all this. I only hope I can eat it all.'

'Me too. I bought far more than I intended, especially as Nathan's away this weekend.' He shook his head. 'You're a bad influence, Eleanor. You're going to have to make amends.'

'How?' Ellie asked in surprise.

'By coming home and having lunch with me, that's how.' He laughed softly, causing a tiny frisson of awareness to ripple through her. 'That way at least some of this stuff won't go to waste. To my mind it's the least you can do for encouraging me to be so greedy!'

Daniel unlocked the front door, still not quite able to believe that Eleanor had agreed to have lunch with him. Even as he had issued the invitation, he had expected her to refuse, yet she hadn't. Had it been guilt at the thought of wasting the food that had spurred her on? Or because she wanted to spend more time with him?

He clamped down on that thought as he made his way inside. Eleanor was parking her car so he left the front door open and headed to the kitchen. Dumping the bags on the table, he turned to watch as she came down the hall. It was obvious that she was taking stock and all of a sudden he was conscious of how little he had done to the place recently. It was years since the house had been decorated and everywhere was starting to look decidedly shabby. He would have to do something about it, although it was odd that it should have taken Eleanor's visit to make him see the place through fresh eyes.

'It's a lovely house,' she said as she came into the kitchen. 'Very warm and welcoming.'

'Thank you. I've always liked it, although it needs a bit of a spruce up,' Daniel replied, pleased that she liked his home even if it wasn't looking its best.

'It's hard to fit everything in when you're working,' she said quietly, but he heard the undercurrent in her voice and knew that she was wondering if he had failed to make any changes because of Camille. Was she right? Had he held off redecorating because he'd wanted everything to remain as it had been in happier times?

He suspected it was true and it was uncomfortable to face up to how he had placed his life on hold. How many times had he counselled a bereaved patient about the importance of looking towards the future and yet he was guilty of ignoring his own advice. He knew that he would have to address the situation and soon. After all, there were going to be a lot of changes when Nathan went to university; he would be here on his own after that.

'Right, first things first—let's get that soup heated up,' he declared, not wanting to dwell on the thought of how lonely he was going to be. 'We can have it with some of that fresh bread and cheese we bought.'

'Let's use some of my cheese,' Eleanor suggested immediately. She grimaced as she slipped off her jacket and hung it on the peg behind the back door. 'I've bought far too much—I'll never manage to eat it all by myself.'

'Fine. There's plates on the dresser and cutlery in the drawer... Oh, and the cheese board's in that cupboard,' Daniel told her as he set about opening the carton of soup.

'Right.' Eleanor started to gather together what they needed, laying out plates and cutlery and even finding the butter dish in the fridge. 'Napkins?' she asked, glancing round, and he grimaced.

'Not sure where they are, to be honest. I do have some but, as I never entertain, I don't use them.'

'Not to worry. This will do.' She tore off a couple of sheets of kitchen roll and folded them neatly into triangles before setting them on the table.

Daniel laughed. 'I'm glad you aren't too fussy.'

'I'm more practical than fussy,' she said, smiling back. Her eyes met his and Daniel felt his heart give a little bounce, as though it had suddenly discovered it had a spring in it. He turned back to the soup, concentrating on stirring it so that it didn't catch on the bottom of the pan. It was just a smile, nothing to get het up about, and certainly nothing to make him think how much he would love her to smile at him again if he kissed her...

A blob of hot soup spat out of the pan and landed on his hand and he jumped but at least it helped to clear his head. By the time the soup was ready and the bread was sliced, he felt back on an even keel. Ladling the soup into a couple of earthenware bowls, he placed them on the table. 'Spiced carrot and coriander. I've not had it before so I hope it tastes good.'

'It's lovely,' Eleanor declared, taking an appreciative sip. She helped herself to a slice of onion bread and buttered it liberally. 'Hmm, this is delicious too.'

'Better than the supermarket's best white sliced?' Daniel asked, his tongue firmly in his cheek.

'*Ye3*' She rolled her eyes. 'Not all of us have been lucky enough to be able to buy such fresh produce. Where I lived before it was the supermarket or nothing.'

'So you aren't sorry you moved here?'

'Not at all.' Ellie hesitated, not sure it was wise to admit how glad she was that she had made the move. It wasn't just the food; her whole outlook on life seemed so much more positive since she had come to the Dales. However, the reason why it felt so much brighter stopped her elaborating. Telling Daniel that meeting him had been a major factor was out of the question.

'Good. It must have been a big decision and I'm glad you don't regret it.'

'I don't.' Eleanor busied herself with her lunch, not wanting to be drawn into saying too much. The problem was that Daniel was so easy to talk to that she found it hard to hold back as she normally would do. She had never been someone who wore her heart on her sleeve: just the opposite. Yet, when she was with Daniel it was as though she wanted to tell him everything—every tiny concern she had, every emotion she was feeling. She had never felt this way before and it was hard to understand how he had this effect on her. What was it about him that breached all her defences?

It was a relief when Daniel changed the subject by telling her about Nathan's trip. That he was extremely proud of his son was obvious and she found it incredibly moving. Although she knew that her parents were proud of what she had achieved, she had never felt that they gained such pleasure from her success as Daniel seemed to derive from Nathan's.

'You're very proud of him, aren't you?'

'Is it that obvious?' Daniel sighed. 'Sorry! I didn't mean to bore you to death by playing the doting parent.'

'You aren't boring me. I think it's great that you two have such a close relationship. Not many parents are as close to their children as you are.'

'It's probably because of what happened,' Daniel said quietly. 'Camille's illness was a testing time for us. After she died, Nathan went completely off the rails. I honestly thought that he'd never get back on track, but in the end he came through. I'm incredibly proud of what he's achieved because it wasn't easy for him.'

'It mustn't have been easy for you either,' Ellie suggested, her heart aching at the thought of what he had been through. She glanced around the kitchen, taking note of the photographs pinned to the cork board above the fridge. There were several family photos, proof that Camille was still very much in his thoughts. 'Dealing with your grief as well as trying to help Nathan must have been very difficult.'

'It was a dark period, but we got through it.' He

smiled, obviously wanting to dispel the sombre mood. 'Now it's time to look to the future, me as well as Nathan.'

'That sounds as though you're planning on making some changes,' Ellie observed.

'I am.' He glanced around the room and shrugged. 'I never realised until today that I've slipped into a bit of a rut. The house desperately needs redecorating and I shall have to do something about it, or even think about moving.'

'Really?' Ellie couldn't hide her surprise. 'It's a beautiful house, though. Maybe it does need updating but that's all, surely?'

'With Nathan about to move out I have to ask myself if I need all this space. We bought this house as our family home but when there's just me rattling around in it, it seems a waste. Moving somewhere smaller might be a good idea.'

'A fresh start,' she suggested, her heart surging at the thought that Daniel was making a positive move toward putting the past behind him.

'Yes.' He looked at her and her breath caught when she saw the expression in his eyes. 'I think it's time to move on, Eleanor. I don't want to live in the past any more. I want a future to look forward to.'

Eleanor didn't know what to say. Did he mean that he wanted her to feature in that future? Just for a moment her mind whirled as she pictured the life they could have. There was no doubt that she found Daniel very attractive. She also found him wonderfully easy to talk to, but was that enough? Surely it needed more than sexual attraction and compatibility to guarantee a life-long relationship? There had to be love as well, a deep abiding love that would withstand everything that life could throw at them. He'd had that with Camille but was it possible to find that kind of closeness with anyone else, or would the other person always be second-best?

Ellie felt a searing pain clutch her chest. She knew how that felt, how dispiriting it was to know that you weren't enough, not number one. Gemma had held the key position in their parents' hearts and Ellie had been aware of that when she had been growing up. That's why meeting Michael had been so wonderful; for the first time ever she had felt she was the most important person in someone's life, but it hadn't lasted. How could she risk that happening again? Why would she choose to put herself through that heartache a second time?

She took a deep breath. Maybe she was attracted to Daniel, as he was to her, but it wasn't enough. Not when he would never love her as he had loved his late wife.

Daniel could feel shock waves reverberating throughout his body. Where on earth had that idea sprung from? he wondered as he got up to make some coffee. One minute he'd been wondering if he should embark on a spot of decorating and the next he'd been thinking about selling up!

As he filled the cafetière he let the idea roam around his head, hoping to find an explanation and preferably one that didn't involve Eleanor. Letting himself think that they might have a future together was crazy. She was only just recovering from a painful experience with her ex and she was in no state to embark on another relationship. Even if she had been it certainly wasn't the right time for him! He knew all that, so all he could do was put it down to some sort of mental aberration, an overload of crazy ideas that had addled his brain.

He placed the coffee pot on the table then took some mugs off the dresser and found the milk and sugar. By the time that was done he had managed to calm himself down. 'Coffee?' he asked, resuming the role of host as it was a much safer option than exploring any more crazy ideas.

'Please.' Eleanor popped the last bit of bread into her mouth and sighed. 'That was delicious. Oh, I know folk go on and on about the meals they've had at all those fancy restaurants but you can't beat what we've just had.'

'I'm glad you enjoyed it. I don't feel so guilty now for egging you on to buy so much,' Daniel declared, rustling up a smile.

'It's my own fault,' she replied, laughing. 'One of the dangers of having eyes bigger than my belly, as mum used to warn me.'

'I can't imagine you needed warning,' he observed lightly. 'You're a perfect weight from what I can tell.'

'Thank you.' She coloured at the compliment. 'I wasn't always, though. I was quite a podgy teenager and mum was worried in case I put on too much weight.'

'Really? Had it something to do with your home circumstances?'

'Yes.' She sighed. 'It wasn't a very happy period in my life and I consoled myself by eating. Fortunately, things improved once I went to university.'

'I'm glad,' he said softly, his heart aching at the thought of the struggle she'd had to find her rightful place in the family dynamics. It made him see just how devastating it must have been for her when she had found her fiancé in bed with another woman. Eleanor had been through the mill and he must never forget that.

They drank their coffee, keeping up a carefully casual conversation. Daniel sensed that she was reluctant to reveal anything more about her past and respected her decision even though he longed to learn all he could about her. When Eleanor announced that it was time she left, it was a relief. Even though he had enjoyed the time they had spent together, he needed to take a step back. He had just unhooked her coat from the back of the door when the telephone rang.

'I'll just get that. Won't be a moment,' he said, hurrying into the hall. Picking up the receiver, he listened while the caller identified herself, a wave of coldness enveloping him as she briskly explained that she was the sister in charge of the Accident and Emergency unit at York. The coach carrying Nathan and his fellow students had been involved in an accident: could Daniel come?

Daniel hung up, his hand shaking so that he had difficulty placing the receiver on its rest. He heard footsteps behind him and turned round, his heart hammering so hard that he thought he was going to pass out.

'What is it? What's happened?' Eleanor took hold of his arm and shook it. 'Daniel, tell me!'

'There's been an accident… Nathan's in hospital,' he managed at last.

'Which hospital?'

'York.'

'Right, we'll go straight there.'

'Oh, but you don't have to come,' he began, but she shook her head.

'There's no way that you can drive in that state. And no way that I'll let you. I'm coming with you, Daniel, whether you like it or not!'

CHAPTER ELEVEN

A AND E WAS frantically busy. It turned out that the coach was just one of several vehicles that had been involved in the collision. Nobody seemed to know what had caused it, but that was less important than how Nathan was. He was currently undergoing a CT scan for a head injury and Ellie knew that Daniel was beside himself with worry.

'It shouldn't be long now until we hear something,' she said, trying to keep up his spirits, although she suspected it was a waste of time. Which parent wouldn't be scared stiff at the thought of their child being injured?

'It seems to be taking ages!' Daniel exploded, leaping up from his seat. They had been shown into the waiting room attached to Resus and he strode to the door and stared through the glass.

'He should have been back by now. Obviously, something's wrong...'

'Or maybe it's just taking that bit longer because of the number of casualties they're having to deal with,' Ellie countered.

'I suppose so,' he conceded, coming back and slumping down in the chair. He ran his hand over his face and she could see that it was trembling. Reaching out, she covered it with hers. She hated seeing him like this—so afraid and filled with angst—but there was little she could do apart from be there and offer her support.

'Sorry. I know I'm behaving like a complete idiot, but I'm just so scared.' He turned his hand over and captured hers. 'I don't know how I'd cope if anything happened to him.'

'I understand. But the registrar said that the CT scan was more a precaution than anything else. He thinks Nathan has a concussion but that it isn't serious,' she reminded him gently.

'He did. But things can and do go wrong when it comes to head injuries...' He broke off and leapt to his feet when the sister appeared and beckoned

to him. Ellie stood up as well, her own heart racing. She may be a doctor but it wasn't easy to
take a balanced view when one knew the people
involved.

'You can come through and see your son now,
Dr Saunders. The CT scan was clear, you'll be
happy to hear.'

'Thank heavens!' Daniel exclaimed. He went to
follow the sister into Resus, pausing when Ellie
stayed where she was. 'Aren't you going to come
with me?'

'If you want me to,' she said uncertainly, not
wanting to intrude.

'Of course I do!' He held the door for her, placing his hand under her elbow as they followed the
sister to a screened-off area in the corner. Nathan
was having his obs done by a young male nurse
so they stood to one side and waited. Although
there was a huge bruise on the side of his face,
Nathan managed to smile at them.

'Hi, Dad… Eleanor. Sorry about this.'

'It's not your fault,' Daniel said gruffly. He went
over to the bed once the nurse had finished and

squeezed Nathan's hand. 'Or at least I don't think it was!'

'Thanks very much!' Nathan laughed then grimaced. He had a broken rib as well as the head injury, although that would heal in its own time, as Ellie knew, and shouldn't cause any major problems.

'So what happened? Do you know?' Daniel asked, sounding better now he knew that Nathan wasn't in any immediate danger.

'Apparently, a tanker overturned and a couple of cars ran into it. We ploughed into the back of the pile-up.'

'Was anyone badly injured from your group?' Daniel asked. 'What about Jack?'

'Not a scratch. He's waiting for Sandra and Tim to collect him. There were a couple of others with bumps and bruises, and one of the girls has a broken wrist, but that's it. We were very lucky.'

'How did you hit your head?' Eleanor asked, curiously.

Nathan sighed. 'I'd just got up to get a can of cola out of my bag when it happened and I went flying. If I'd been sitting down then I'd have been OK.'

'Typical, although it could have been worse.' Daniel squeezed the boy's shoulder. 'Thank heaven it wasn't is all I can say.'

'Me too.'

Ellie felt a lump come to her throat as father and son exchanged a look. There was no doubt that they knew exactly how much they meant to each other. It was hard to tamp down her emotions so she excused herself when the registrar came to speak to Daniel. At the end of the day, they weren't her family, even though she would have loved to be part of their lives. The thought shocked her so much that it was hard to dismiss it when Daniel came to find her a short time later.

'They're going to keep him in overnight. It's purely a precaution—they're not anticipating any problems. But they'd prefer to cover all bases.'

'So what are you going to do?' Ellie asked, trying to get herself together. There was no chance of her becoming a permanent part of Daniel's family and it was pointless thinking that she could.

His life was mapped out and, to put it bluntly, she didn't feature in his plans. 'Are you going to stay here or go home?'

'There's not much point in my staying. Nathan is being moved to a ward soon and he needs to rest.' He glanced at his watch and frowned. 'Is that really the time? I had no idea it was so late. No, I'll go home and come back tomorrow morning to pick him up.'

'Sounds like a good idea,' she agreed. She led the way to the car park, shivering as rain gusted across the open ground as they left the building. 'It's so cold, much colder than when we arrived.'

'Winter's on its way. It'll get colder than this in a few weeks' time.'

'What a cheering thought!' she exclaimed, and he laughed.

'Sorry!'

They got into the car and drove back to Beesdale. Ellie took her time, not wanting to risk them having an accident as well. The roads were slick with rain and with the wind blowing more rain against the windscreen it was difficult to see. It was a relief to pull up outside Daniel's house.

'Come in and have a cup of tea,' he instructed, forcing the door open as the wind tried to slam it shut. 'You've had nothing since lunchtime and you must need a drink.'

'I really should get off home,' she demurred, not sure it would be wise to prolong her stay. Far too many crazy thoughts had invaded her head today and she needed to be on her own while she got things straight again. She must never forget that she was only here for a limited period of time and after that she would move on.

'Please.' Bending, he looked at her through the half-open door and she couldn't fail to see the plea in his eyes. 'I could really do with some company, Eleanor. What happened today really shook me up.'

'In that case a cup of tea would be very welcome.'

Ellie got out of the car, unable to resist the appeal for support. From what she knew, Daniel didn't ask for help very often. Rain lashed at them as they ran up the path and he grimaced as he let them into the house.

'What a night! You're soaked. Go into the sitting room while I fetch you a towel.'

He ushered her inside, pausing only long enough to light the gas fire before he went to find the towel. Ellie took off her wet coat and draped it over the back of a chair then sat down next to the fireplace, holding her hands out to the blaze. He came back a few seconds later with a towel and handed it to her.

'Here you are. I'll pop the kettle on and be right back.'

Ellie started to rub her hair dry as he disappeared again. With it being so short, it didn't take very long. She could have done with combing it afterwards but she hadn't thought to put a comb in her bag when she had set out that morning. She did her best, using her fingers to smooth the short dark strands into some semblance of order. Daniel came back with a tray of tea as she was checking her appearance in the mirror and grinned at her.

'You've missed a bit.'

'Have I?' Turning her head, she attempted to find the wayward strands but couldn't spot them.

'Just here.' Daniel placed the tray on a table and came up behind her. Lifting his hand, he smoothed down the tufts of hair and Ellie stiffened when she felt his fingers sliding down her skull. She bit her lip as she waited for him to move away but he stayed right where he was. 'Your hair is beautiful, Eleanor, so soft and silky.'

His deep voice rippled through the silence, the words charged with so much emotion that she shivered. When his hand returned to her hair, she didn't move. Couldn't. It was as though his touch had cast a spell over her. When his fingers came to rest on the nape of her neck and began to stroke it too, she closed her eyes, letting the sensations pour through her. She could feel her skin tingling, feel the heat building wherever his fingers touched, and sighed. She knew that she should stop what was happening but it was beyond her. How could she call a halt when it felt so good to be touched this way, so right?

'Eleanor?'

There was a question in his voice when he said her name and even though he didn't say it out loud, she knew what he was asking. Her heart caught, panic and excitement bringing it to a halt. All she had to do was to say no and that would be the end of the matter, but for some reason it seemed like the hardest thing she had ever been asked to do. If she refused then she had a feeling that she would always regret it, always wonder what she had missed.

She turned to face him, watching the firelight playing over the strong planes of his face. When he bent towards her, she kept her eyes open, wanting to remember every second of what was happening. Whether it was the shock of Nathan's accident that was responsible for what was happening, she had no idea, but she needed to store away the memory of this moment. It would be something to look back on, something to cherish. His lips were so gentle as they settled over hers and yet beneath the tenderness there was a hunger that shook her. Daniel wasn't kissing her because he was seeking comfort. He was kissing her because he wanted her!

Daniel felt desire surge inside him and gasped. In the space of a heartbeat the kiss had gone from a need for closeness to something far more urgent. He drew Eleanor to him, shuddering when he felt her breasts pushing against his chest. It was a long time since he had been this close to a woman. Camille had been so ill that lovemaking had been out of the question. Now his senses seemed to be swamped by the feel and shape of the woman in his arms.

He drew her closer, marvelling at the fact that they fitted so perfectly. It was as though each curve and hollow had been created so that it would accommodate the shape of the other. Eleanor was quite tall, just a couple of inches shorter than him, and her head rested so comfortably in the crook of his shoulder, the perfect angle to allow him to deepen the kiss. His mouth plundered hers, tasting, testing, savouring the sweetness of her lips. When his tongue began to explore the delicate curve of her mouth, she moaned, the tiniest sound imaginable, but unmistakable all the same.

Daniel shuddered as a wave of desire swept over him. The fact that he was responsible for causing her this pleasure was a heady feeling and he did it again, letting the tip of his tongue trace the perfect curve of her upper lip and the tantalising fullness of her lower one. Her mouth was beautiful, so beautiful that he could have stood there and kissed her for ever and a day, but there were more delights to explore.

His hands slid down her body, skimming over the slender curves. He had never touched her this way before and yet there was a strange sense of familiarity, of rightness, that shook him. Had he unconsciously imagined doing this, pictured himself exploring her body and getting to know its shape and feel? He knew it was true and it was a revelation to realise that she had got under his skin to such an extent. He hadn't realised he was so vulnerable where Eleanor was concerned.

Fear suddenly rose to the surface of his mind as he wondered if he was making a mistake, but then she moved, just slightly, and his seeking hand came to rest on the side of her breast. Daniel felt a red-hot flame of desire shoot through him as his hand stilled for a moment before it moved on, sliding down from her breast to her waist then onto the softly rounded curve of her hip as he drew her closer and let her see the effect her nearness was having on him. Maybe he should have tried to hide what he was feeling but he didn't have the strength.

'Daniel...'

His name was little more than a rush of air as it escaped her lips, but it was nonetheless potent for that. Daniel felt a tremor pass through him. There was such hunger in the sound that he could almost taste it, such need that he was overwhelmed. This wasn't all down to him and *his* needs: Eleanor wanted him too. When he took her hand and led her to the door, she didn't hesitate, and his heart swelled with joy. Why should they pretend that this wasn't what they both wanted?

Light spilled into the room from the landing, just a pale glimmer, but it was enough. Eleanor stood at the end of the bed and waited as Daniel reached out to her. His hands were trembling as he drew the sweater over her head but she understood. He hadn't planned this; it had simply happened. It was little wonder he felt so shocked. She did too.

He dropped her sweater onto the floor then reached for the hem of the T-shirt she wore beneath. That too was quickly dispensed with. Eleanor watched as his eyes grazed over her breasts, barely concealed by the lacy bra she was wearing. When they rose to her face his pupils were dilated, filled with so many emotions that she couldn't have put a name to half of them and didn't try. She didn't need to wonder what he was feeling when she felt it too.

'You're beautiful. So very beautiful.'

The words stroked along her flesh like a caress and she shuddered. When he unfastened the snap on her jeans and started to slide them off her hips she closed her eyes. She didn't need to watch what he was doing now when she could feel it—feel his hands trembling, feel the touch of his fingers smoothing the fabric down her thighs. Bending, he cupped her foot in his hand and eased off first one leg of her jeans and then the other. All she had on now was her underwear and she waited, wondering when—not if—he would remove that as well, but instead he gathered her into his arms and held her close, held her so that she could feel exactly what her nearness was doing to him.

'I want you so much,' he whispered hoarsely. 'I want to hold you, touch you, be inside you, but are you sure it's what you want? It isn't too late if you want me to stop…'

'I don't.' Her voice was firm, her gaze steady as she opened her eyes and looked at him. She didn't want there to be any mistake about what she was saying, didn't intend for there to be room for re-criminations later. Daniel wanted to make love to her and it was what she wanted too. Maybe there would be regrets at some point—who knew? But at this moment it was what she wanted. Needed. Desperately.

He closed his eyes, almost as though the moment was too intense to bear, and maybe it was.

This was a big step for both of them and it would be foolish to pretend that it didn't mean anything. When he held out his hand, she took it and let him lead her to the bed. Kissing her softly on the mouth, he eased her down onto the quilt then straightened. Stripping off his sweater and jeans, he tossed them onto the floor and lay down beside her, drawing her into his arms so that she could feel the heat of his skin seeping into her flesh. His body was hard and firm, its shape and feel so new and so different; there was so much to discover.

Ellie let her fingertips graze over the well-developed pectoral muscles, feeling the crispness of hair and the smoothness of the skin beneath. Daniel's shoulders were broad and her fingers skated along his collar bones until they reached the tips then retraced their route, coming to rest above his heart. She could feel its beat beneath her palm, feel the blood surging, the power of his life-force, and realised that she had never felt this close to anyone before. Right here, at this moment, she could feel his heart pounding, and it was pounding for her.

Her hands moved on, grazing lightly over his rib cage, the firm flat muscles in his abdomen until she came to his hips. He was fully aroused and she took him into her hands, feeling the power, the proof of his need for her. She had never taken the lead when making love before and yet she didn't hesitate as she stroked and caressed him. This was different from anything she had experienced before. This was Daniel.

'Eleanor!' His voice rasped harshly as he cried out her name. Rolling her over onto her back, he kissed her with a passion that made her head swirl. Drawing back, he stared into her eyes and she could feel him trembling with the force of his feelings. 'I don't have anything,' he murmured. 'Nothing to keep you safe...'

'It's all right,' she said softly, moved almost beyond bearing that he should worry about protecting her at such a moment. 'I'm still on the Pill.'

He didn't say anything, simply kissed her with great tenderness as he entered her. Eleanor felt her body open to allow him in, felt it close around him and hold him there. There was no fumbling, no wondering what to do. It was instinctive, as though they had had been created for this very purpose. They climaxed together, shivering, shuddering, and utterly sated as they slid back down to earth. Daniel cupped her cheek in his hand and she could see the wonder in his eyes.

'I never thought…' he began then broke off as though he found it impossible to describe his feelings.

'No,' she agreed, her voice trembling from the aftermath of what had happened. 'Neither did I.'

He didn't say a word as he drew her to him and Ellie felt tears come to her eyes. He understood how she felt, how shocked she was, how moved, because he felt the same way. When he started to caress her again, she immersed herself in the magic they were creating. This time their lovemaking was slow and tender but just as intense. She had never experienced this kind of closeness and rapport. It was a world away from mere desire and touched on realms that scared her. She didn't want to fall in love with Daniel—she wouldn't take that risk. She couldn't bear to have her heart broken again, especially when she knew that it would be so much worse this time.

Ellie bit her lip as euphoria faded and was replaced by fear. If she allowed herself to love Daniel then there would be no holding back, no reservations, no safeguards. She would have to give him her heart and every tiny bit of her being. She would have nothing left if he rejected her.

CHAPTER TWELVE

DANIEL COULD FEEL the shock waves reverberating throughout his entire body. It felt as though he had undergone some kind of traumatic evolution, everything he knew and understood ripped apart and put back together in a different order. Making love to Eleanor had changed him from the man he had been. It was no wonder that he felt so disorientated.

When Eleanor pulled away, he let her go. He needed to get his thoughts together and he couldn't do that while he held her. He rolled to his feet, feeling sick as he wondered where they went from here. Maybe they had gone into this with their eyes open, but how must she be feeling? he thought as he dragged on his jeans. She was still struggling to come to terms with what had happened with her ex and now to be faced with this!

Guilt rushed through him as he picked up his sweater, guilt about how Eleanor was feeling as well as guilt about what he himself had done. He hadn't thought about Camille—she hadn't entered his mind once. However, there was no point pretending that he wasn't going to feel guilty about betraying her memory when he knew that he would.

'I'll make us a drink,' he said roughly, avoiding looking at Eleanor. Maybe she had been a willing participant but she hadn't thought through what they were doing any more than he had done.

Daniel took a deep breath and tried to damp down a surge of remorse. Blaming desire for his actions wasn't acceptable. He should have thought about what he was doing and not allowed himself to be influenced by his needs. The funny thing was that he had never been led by his emotions before, but it was different with Eleanor; he felt more and thought less.

'The bathroom's through there if you want a shower,' he said, trying not to dwell on that thought. 'I'll make us some coffee.'

'Thank you.'

Her voice was low, the uncertainties it held tugging at his heartstrings, but he forced himself to ignore them. After all, people slept together all the time and it didn't have to make a huge impact on their lives, did it? However, in his heart, he knew that dismissing what they had done wasn't going to be easy. Like it or not, it was going to have an effect.

His heart was heavy as he made his way downstairs and switched on the kettle. It was pitch-dark outside and all he could see through the kitchen window was his own reflection staring back at him. It was like looking at the face of a stranger. This morning he had known exactly who he was: Daniel Saunders, widower, father, doctor, a man who lived his life the best way he could. Now it felt as though he was someone completely different and he hadn't a clue who he was any more. It was as though all the certainties that had shaped his life had melted away and there was no framework any more. He could be whoever he wanted but the hard part was deciding who that was.

'I think I should go.'

Daniel swung round when Eleanor spoke. She was fully dressed and he experienced a rush of regret that he could no longer enjoy looking at her beautiful body but he squashed it. He needed to sort out his head and thoughts like that wouldn't help him do that. 'Are you sure you won't stay and have a cup of coffee?' he said politely.

'Thank you, but no.' She stood up straighter and he could tell that she was steeling herself to continue. 'About tonight, Daniel, I think it's best if we forget what happened.'

'Do you think that's possible?' he asked wryly, and she flushed.

'It won't be easy, but it's the sensible thing to do, unless, of course, you'd prefer me to leave the surgery.'

'No. That's the last thing I want,' he said quickly, his heart sinking at the thought. He took a deep breath, struggling to retain his composure. 'We're both adults, Eleanor, and we both understand that these things happen. Put it down to an emotional overload after what happened today, but there's no point us making a song and dance about it. Bluntly, I'd find it very difficult to replace you at this time of the year so I'd appreciate it if you would stay on.'

'I would prefer not to have to find another position right now too so it's fine with me.' She gave him a quick smile although Daniel was very aware how empty it was. 'I'll be happy to stay. Thank you.'

She didn't say anything else. Daniel followed her into the hall, aware that he had handled things badly. He didn't want her to think he was dismissing what had happened between them as meaningless but what else could he have done? The fact was that Eleanor had made it clear that she wouldn't welcome it if he told her just how much tonight had meant to him.

She fetched her coat from the sitting room and went to the door. 'I hope Nathan makes a speedy recovery,' she said, glancing back. 'If you need anything—'

'Thank you but you did more than enough today,' he interjected swiftly.

'I was glad to help.'

Her eyes met his for a moment before she turned round and opened the front door but it was long enough. Daniel's hands clenched when he saw the pain they held. That she regretted what had happened tonight was obvious. He longed to say something to make it easier for her but the words wouldn't come. He couldn't make any declarations or promises, could he? Maybe the boundaries within which he lived his life had altered, but some things were exactly the same. He was still Nathan's father and now, more than ever, he needed to put him first.

Ellie was dreading seeing Daniel when she went into work on Monday morning but, in the event, he wasn't there. It appeared that Nathan had been kept in hospital and Daniel had taken the day off to be with him. Marie sounded concerned as she relayed the news to her.

'Apparently, Nathan started complaining of a headache then lost consciousness. They did another scan and discovered a bleed on his brain and decided to operate. They phoned Daniel and he went rushing back to the hospital in the early hours of Sunday morning.'

'Good heavens!' Ellie exclaimed. 'Nathan seemed fine when I saw him. There was no indication that something like that would happen.'

'You were at the hospital!' Marie exclaimed in surprise.

'Yes.' Ellie could feel herself blushing as she recalled what had happened on Saturday night. She had spent the rest of the weekend vacillating between trying to forget it and remembering every single glorious second. She had never imagined that she and Daniel would end up in bed together. That had been a big enough shock; however, the fact that their lovemaking had been so wonderful made it even more alarming. She knew that she couldn't simply ignore what had happened. She was going to have to live with the memory... If she could.

'I...erm... I ran into Daniel at the market,' she said, opting for part of the truth. 'We got a bit carried away and ended up buying so much food that he invited me back to his for lunch so it wouldn't get wasted. I was there when the hospital phoned to say Nathan was in A and E and I drove Daniel over there.'

'I see.' Marie was obviously agog to hear more and Ellie swiftly moved on.

'As I said, Nathan seemed fine when we left so it's a shock to hear what's happened. But there again head injuries are notoriously difficult to spot.'

'I suppose so. What time did you and Daniel get back to Beesdale?' Marie asked, not to be deterred.

'Oh, not too late. Anyway, how is Nathan doing?' Ellie said quickly.

'All right, apparently. Daniel phoned me just after seven this morning to tell me what had happened and that he wouldn't be at work,' Marie explained, successfully distracted. 'He'd already phoned Sandra and asked her to cover for him so she should be here shortly.' Marie grimaced. 'No doubt Bernard will have a face on him because he'll be on his own, but tough. It's about time he actually did some work!'

Ellie laughed as Marie rolled her eyes. Fortunately, their first patient arrived just then so she was able to make her escape. However, as she went into her room, she made herself take a deep breath. It was time to put what had happened out of her mind and focus on work, although she knew it would be only a temporary reprieve. It would be a long time before she forgot about making love with Daniel.

Daniel could feel tiredness dragging at him. He hadn't slept since he had arrived at the hospital in the early hours of Sunday morning. Even though he had been assured that the operation had been a complete success, he had stayed awake, watching over his son. Nathan had been moved to the Critical Care unit, an indication that his status had changed for the worse. Although Daniel knew that he was receiving the best possible care, he wouldn't relax until Nathan regained consciousness. He had been heavily sedated to give his brain a chance to heal and it could take some time before that happened. Meanwhile, Daniel intended to stay at his bedside. Sandra would cover for him and Eleanor would be there as well.

His heart jolted at the thought of what had gone on in the past forty-eight hours. First Nathan's accident and then him and Eleanor making love. Maybe the first event had been the catalyst for the second but deep down he knew it would have happened at some point. Ever since they had met, he had felt drawn to Eleanor. He'd only ever felt this way once before, when he had met Camille, but even then it had been different. He and Camille had been so young when they had met and fallen in love. They'd had their whole lives ahead of them and being in love had been wild and exciting. With Eleanor, however, the feeling was different, quieter, deeper, more intense in a way. Was he falling in love with her? He didn't know. All he knew was that he wanted to be with her and not just in bed either.

Thoughts tumbled around his head. They were intermingled with so many emotions, guilt being the main one. How could he fall in love with Eleanor when it would mean him letting go of Camille? He had sworn to love Camille until his dying day and he would have done so too if he'd had the chance. But would it be right to allow himself to love someone else? Or would it be a rejection of everything he and Camille had had together?

Then there was Nathan; how would *he* feel about his father loving another woman? The last thing Daniel wanted was to upset Nathan, especially now when his son had this to contend with. He had already let Nathan down by leaving him in the hospital on his own. Oh, maybe he couldn't have done anything to prevent what had happened but he should have been here, taking care of him, rather than satisfying his own needs. It was something he had no intention of doing again.

He took a deep breath. He and Eleanor could never have a relationship, no matter how much he might want to.

Ellie was kept extremely busy all morning long. The plus side was that she had no time to brood about what had happened. She had just ushered out her final patient when Marie buzzed to tell her that there was a Dr Margaret Hamilton on the phone, wanting to speak to Daniel, but would she take the call seeing as he wasn't there.

'Of course,' Ellie agreed immediately. She listened carefully as Dr Hamilton introduced herself. It appeared she was a psychotherapist and worked with both private patients as well as those referred to her through NHS channels.

'I am extremely concerned about a patient who is on your list. Her name is Madeleine Walsh— I don't know if you've been involved in her care, Dr Munroe?'

'In an indirect way, yes, I have, although she is Dr Saunders' patient.' Ellie quickly explained about Nigel Walsh's visit and heard the other woman sigh.

'Oh, there's no doubt that she's self-harming, or that it's spiralling out of control. I've only seen her the once but it was obvious that she urgently needs counselling. The problem is that she's failed to attend the last two appointments I set up for her.' Margaret Hamilton sounded worried. 'Letters and phone calls have been ignored too, which is why I was hoping that Dr Saunders could have a word with her. Madeleine knows him and he might just be able to make her see how important it is that she gets the help she needs.'

'I'm sure he would be happy to speak to her,' Ellie said slowly, hoping that she wasn't making too many assumptions. Daniel had had his doubts about the situation but now that Dr Hamilton was involved, surely it would allay his concerns? She hurried on. 'However, his son is in hospital at the moment, which is why he isn't in today, and I'm not sure when he will be back. I could have a word with Mrs Walsh if you think it would help, although, as I said, I don't know her personally. I'd hate to do more harm than good by jumping in,' she added.

'Hm. That's a valid point. People who self-harm are reluctant to admit to what they do at the best of times. Madeleine could respond adversely if you confront her and that's something I want to avoid.' Dr Hamilton paused, obviously weighing up their options. 'I think it would be best to wait until Dr Saunders returns.'

Ellie hung up after they had said goodbye. Although she wasn't happy about the delay, the last thing she wanted was to create more problems for the patient. She brought up Madeleine Walsh's file and made a note on it to the effect that Dr Hamilton had expressed concern then emailed a copy to Daniel so that he would see it when he returned. When that would be was open to question. It all depended on Nathan and how swiftly he recovered. Or didn't.

Ellie's heart contracted. Now that she had met Nathan she felt personally involved. He was Daniel's son, after all, and she couldn't bear to think that he might not recover from his injuries. Tears suddenly welled to her eyes. She couldn't bear to imagine how Daniel would cope if anything happened to the boy.

Nathan finally regained consciousness at lunchtime the following day. Daniel had been warned that he might have difficulty remembering what had happened and not expect too much. This type of head injury often resulted in memory loss and no one could predict if Nathan would be affected by it. Nathan's initial response seemed to confirm his worst fears.

'What's going on, Dad? What am I doing here?'

'You had a bit of a bump on Saturday when you were on that field trip,' Daniel explained carefully. 'You hit your head so they brought you to the hospital.'

'Really?' Nathan looked around in astonishment. 'I don't remember anything about it. What happened?'

'The coach you were on was involved in a pile-up,' Daniel replied, keeping it brief as the consultant had told him to do.

'Weird. The last thing I remember is talking to you and Eleanor at the barbecue—how odd is that?'

'It can happen sometimes when you've had a knock on the head,' Daniel replied lightly, although he had a bad feeling about this.

'S'pose.' Nathan frowned. 'Is Eleanor here? I have this funny feeling that I was talking to her.'

'You're right—she was here,' Daniel agreed, feeling slightly better now that Nathan was starting to piece things together.

'I thought so!' Nathan sounded relieved. 'So where's she gone then?'

'Oh…er…ahem… She went to fetch some coffee,' Daniel replied then wished he had thought of something else to say. Nathan obviously had no concept of time and was going to wonder what was going on when Eleanor failed to appear.

'Good idea. I could do with a cup. I'm parched!'

'No coffee for you, young man. You're getting water.' Daniel filled the plastic beaker and inserted a drinking straw through the spout. Nathan grinned when he passed it to him.

'It's been a while since I had a straw!'

Daniel chuckled, heartened by the fact that Nathan seemed to be taking things in his stride. The last thing he wanted was him getting stressed when it would make the situation even more difficult. 'I'll buy you a pack next time I go shopping.'

'Hmm, tempting, although I'm not sure it would do much for my street cred.' Nathan drank thirstily then sank back against the pillows with a sigh. 'I'm knackered. D'you mind if I have a sleep? Eleanor can keep you company when she gets back with the coffee, can't she?'

'Erm…yes.' Daniel waited until Nathan's eyes closed then left the room, feeling in a quandary. Nathan would think it very odd if Eleanor wasn't there when he woke up and he wasn't sure what to do. The consultant had been adamant about him keeping everything as normal as possible so as not to put any pressure on Nathan, so maybe he should phone Eleanor and ask if she would come to the hospital?

Daniel's heart lurched. Part of him was desperate to have her there with him while the other part was just as desperate for her to stay away. If he was brutally honest, he wasn't sure he could trust himself not to do something stupid when he saw her. Nathan's relapse had shocked him to the core and his emotions were all over the place. The last thing he wanted was a repeat of what had happened on Saturday night.

It was hard to know what to do but in the end the need to make things appear as normal as possible for Nathan's sake won through. He went outside to make the call, sheltering from the rain in the porch. When Eleanor answered he steeled himself to sound as impersonal as possible. This wasn't for his benefit, he told himself sternly. It was to help Nathan and he had to make that clear from the outset. He couldn't afford to let Eleanor know how much he wanted her there—it wouldn't be fair.

Eleanor had just let herself into the flat when her phone rang. Hunting it out of her pocket, she felt her breath catch when she realised it was Daniel calling. Just for a moment she considered rejecting the call before she thought better of it. Daniel wouldn't be calling unless it was urgent.

'Hello?'

'Look, I'm really sorry to phone you like this, Eleanor, but I have a problem.' Daniel's tone was brisk. 'Nathan has regained consciousness but he doesn't remember what happened leading up to the operation. I was warned this could happen and that under no circumstances must I try to jog his memory.'

'I can see how worrying it must be,' she agreed, her heart going out to him.

'It is. He thought it was still Friday, straight after the barbecue. He does recall talking to you, however, because he asked where you'd gone.' She heard him sigh. 'I don't know why but I told him you'd gone for some coffee. It was a really stupid thing to do as Nathan immediately latched onto it. I know it's a lot to ask but is there any chance that you would drive over here? I just want to make things as normal as possible for him.'

Ellie wasn't sure what to do. If it would help Nathan then of course she would drive to the hospital. However, was it really wise to get more deeply involved in Daniel's affairs when she should be trying to keep her distance? She hesitated and Daniel obviously misinterpreted her silence.

'Look, I'm sorry. I should never have phoned you, Eleanor. It was a really bad idea,' he began.'

'I'll come straight over,' she said, cutting him off. She would never forgive herself if she refused to go and something happened to Nathan.

'Are you sure?' The relief in Daniel's voice was like balm and helped to calm her nerves.

'Quite sure. Where exactly are you?'

'Critical Care. I'll tell them to expect you so just give your name in at the desk when you arrive.'

'Right. I should be there within the hour,' Ellie told him, opening the front door.

'Thank you. I really appreciate this.'

Ellie didn't say anything as she cut the connection and headed out to her car. Maybe it wasn't the most sensible decision she'd ever made but she wouldn't go back on it now. She drove out of the surgery, forcing herself to concentrate on the road rather than the mistake she might be making. Daniel had asked her to help his son and she couldn't refuse. It was as simple as that.

CHAPTER THIRTEEN

ELEANOR ARRIVED AT the Critical Care unit just as Nathan was waking up from his nap. He grinned when he saw her coming into the room.

'Hi, Eleanor. Good to know the old man's had some company while I've been doing my sleeping beauty routine.'

'I'm not sure the beauty bit is correct,' she retorted, deliberately keeping her tone light. 'That's some bruise you've got on your head, young man!' She glanced at Daniel and felt her stomach sink when she saw his expression. That he had misgivings about her being there was obvious, even though it had been his idea to ask her to come. For some reason the thought annoyed her so that her voice had a definite edge when she addressed him. 'What do you think, Daniel?'

'I've seen worse,' he replied rather curtly.

'He certainly has.' Nathan laughed. 'Remember the time the shed roof gave way when I was trying to get my football? I ended up with a massive bruise on my head. Mum tore a strip off you for letting me climb up there to fetch it.'

'Mum hauled me over the coals, all right. She said *I* should have gone up and got it even though the roof would never have held my weight.' Daniel rolled his eyes. 'Apparently, that would have been a much better option in her view than you getting hurt.'

'I remember,' Nathan replied, grinning. 'You were seriously not impressed!'

Ellie turned away, trying not to think about what a happy family they had been. It simply highlighted how devastating it must have been for them when Camille had died. How could anyone hope to replace Camille let alone replicate the kind of closeness they'd had? It was hard to put that thought out of her mind, even though she knew how stupid it was to dwell on it. Daniel hadn't asked her to come here so she could step into his late wife's shoes. Nobody could fill Camille's role in either Daniel's or Nathan's eyes, and any woman who tried would only ever be second best. It was such a painful thought it was relief when the consultant arrived to examine Nathan and they were asked to leave. At least it provided a breathing space, time to get herself together. Daniel might have asked for her help for Nathan's sake but that was all.

They stepped out into the corridor while they waited for the consultant to finish. Daniel sighed as he stared at the closed door. 'The longer the amnesia lasts, the less likely it is that he'll recover that part of his memory.'

'I thought you said that he'd remembered us being at the barbecue and me being here on Saturday,' Ellie said quietly, her heart aching for what he must have been going through.

'Yes, although I'm not sure he has the time scale exactly right.' He ran his hand through his hair, his face grey with a mixture of fatigue and tension. 'And what if there are other gaps in his memory and we know nothing about them? They might only surface later on.'

'There's nothing to say that's going to happen, Daniel,' she pointed out firmly. 'Nathan could remember everything else perfectly well.'

'Or he might have forgotten something important, maybe something to do with his college work.' His tone was grim. 'He's worked so damned hard to get his act together. If something like that happens then heaven knows the effect it could have on him.'

'Don't go borrowing trouble, as my grandma used to say,' she instructed. 'It's all ifs, ands and buts at the moment. There are no facts to base your assumptions on, are there?'

'No,' he said slowly, then grimaced. 'Sorry. I'm getting several steps ahead of myself, aren't I?'

'Yes. But it's understandable.' She touched his hand then realised immediately what a mistake it was when she felt a rush of awareness hit her. All of a sudden she was transported back to Saturday night, to how his skin had felt when she had touched him, and how his body had throbbed for hers. Her hand fell to her side but she could tell from his expression that he knew what she was thinking, feeling, knew because he was thinking and feeling it too. The thought shook her. It hadn't ended on Saturday night. What had started then was still going on. The question now was what should she do about it? Assuming that she had a choice.

Daniel could feel the tension sizzling in the air. One minute he had been totally consumed by worry over Nathan and the next he was awash with feelings he didn't know how to handle. When the door opened and the consultant asked them if they would come in, it took him a moment to respond. However, one glimpse of Nathan's face soon cleared his head. His son looked scared to death.

'Did you know that I've got a gap in my memory?' Nathan demanded as soon as they stepped into the room.

'I suspected you had,' Daniel replied as evenly as he could. He glanced at the consultant, who nodded as though giving him permission to continue. 'What exactly do you remember?'

'I remember the barbecue and talking to you both there. And I have this vague impression of Eleanor being here at the hospital—' Nathan broke off and gulped. 'I don't remember anything after that—passing out, going down to Theatre—none of it. It's as though the days are all muddled up. I thought it was still Friday but the doctor says it's Tuesday. Is that right?'

'Yes.' Daniel tried to sound reassuring, although it wasn't easy when Nathan's obvious distress was affecting him. 'It's quite normal to forget things after a head injury. More often than not the missing bits come back later.'

'But what if they don't come back? And what if I've forgotten other things and don't *know* I've forgotten them?' Nathan was sounding increasingly alarmed, which was the last thing Daniel wanted.

'Then they may come back as well.' Eleanor stepped forward, bending so that she could look into the boy's eyes. 'It's early days, Nathan. You've just had surgery and, like any other part of your body, your brain needs time to recover. The best thing you can do is rest and try not to worry, although I can see how hard that must be.'

The advice had an instant soothing effect. Daniel was overcome with gratitude when he saw Nathan relax just a little. Somehow, Eleanor had managed to calm him down, succeeding where he himself had failed. By the time the consultant had added his endorsement to Eleanor's advice, Nathan was looking a lot better. When the sister informed them it was time they left so that Nathan could rest, Daniel felt calmer too. Maybe this wasn't going to turn out as badly as he had feared thanks to Eleanor. They left the Critical Care unit and made their way to the car park. Eleanor had parked next to him and Daniel stopped when they reached her car, aware that everything he was feeling must be clear to see on his face.

'Thank you for what you did back there. You managed to do what I couldn't and calmed him down. I don't know what would have happened if you hadn't been here tonight, Eleanor.'

'You'd have managed.' She smiled up at him, her eyes filled with a tenderness that touched his heart. That she cared not only about Nathan but about him as well was clear to see.

'Maybe,' he said huskily. 'But sometimes managing by yourself isn't enough. Sometimes you need someone to help you.'

He drew her into his arms, feeling the softness of her body nestled against his. It felt like a homecoming, that he had found the place he wanted to be as well the person he wanted to fill it. Holding Eleanor in his arms, he felt whole, as though he was no longer missing some vital part of him. It was a revelation to realise it and yet it was a quiet revelation; it didn't need a fanfare to herald its arrival when it filled him with such an intense feeling of happiness.

Tilting her chin, he kissed her, unable to hold back when every fibre of his being demanded an even greater closeness. He needed her so much! Needed her to fill his heart, his life, to give him peace. When she kissed him back, he could have shouted out for joy only his mouth was too busy to waste a single precious second when it could be better employed. The kiss ran on and on so that they were both trembling when they drew apart, both aware that they had reached a point of no return. They couldn't go back. They could only go forward. Whichever way it led.

'Will you come home with me?' Daniel didn't try to couch his needs in euphemisms—there was no point. They both knew what he was asking so why bother? Eleanor looked into his eyes and he knew what she was going to say before the words left her lips, and shuddered. She wasn't going to pretend either.

'Yes.'

They spent the night at the flat. It wasn't a conscious decision to stay there because they didn't discuss it; it just felt right. Here, at the newly decorated flat that held no reminders of the past, they were free to be themselves. When Daniel took her in his arms, Ellie knew that it was what she wanted more than anything. Maybe she didn't know what the future held in store, but at that moment *this* was what she needed, Daniel's arms around her, his heart beating in time with hers.

They made love with an intensity and passion that moved them both to tears but they weren't embarrassed by their feelings, by the fact that they cared. Even if they didn't know what was going to happen, they needed this, needed each other.

They fell asleep still wrapped in each other's arms and woke the next morning way before the day had dawned, feeling both sated and content. Raising herself up on her elbow, Ellie brushed a kiss over Daniel's brow. 'That was the best night's sleep I've had in ages,' she told him, smiling into his eyes. 'You, Dr Saunders, have a magical touch.'

'Hmm. Good to know, although I suspect the magic only works for selected people.' He brushed her mouth with a kiss, kissed her again when she responded, and groaned. 'I could do this all day. I just wish I had the time but I need to go home and get changed. I want to get to the hospital early to see how Nathan's doing this morning.'

'Of course you do,' Ellie agreed, simply, because no way was she going to put pressure on him to stay with her. Nathan's health was his number one priority and everything came second to that, herself included. Just for a moment the old thoughts about being second best came rushing back before she drove them out of her mind. Daniel needed her help, he needed her support, and no matter what it cost her, she would give it to him.

They showered together, laughing and giggling like teenagers as they squeezed into the stall. When Daniel offered to soap her back, Ellie agreed because it was easier than trying to do it herself. However, it soon became apparent that his interest wasn't wholly focused on matters of hygiene. She shuddered when she felt his hands smoothing the lather over her buttocks. Everywhere he touched, her skin was tingling. When he turned her around and lathered her breasts, she closed her eyes, too awash with sensations to remonstrate with him. They made love again right there in the shower, the water raining down on them as they loved each other with a desperation that was in total contrast to the night before. However, it was equally stirring, equally moving in its own very special way. They wanted one another. Needed one another. And there was no escaping that fact.

Daniel left after downing a quick cup of coffee, leaving Ellie to get ready for work. She dressed with care, suddenly wishing that she had something prettier to wear than the sensible trousers and shirt. She sighed as she studied her reflection in the dressing table mirror, understanding only too well why she wanted to look attractive. She wanted this—whatever it was—to continue, but would it? Could it? Should it? Daniel hadn't made any promises. He hadn't made a commitment either. He had held her, loved her and shown that he'd needed her, but that was all.

Ellie bit her lip as she looked at herself in the mirror. She might be what he needed right now, at this moment, but there was no guarantee his feelings would last. She must never allow herself to forget that.

It was the strangest time of Daniel's entire life. As one week flowed into the next, he found himself adrift. Nathan had been moved to the neurosurgical unit and he spent as much time as possible there with him. Amazingly, Bernard Hargreaves had come up trumps for once, which meant he could take time off without feeling guilty. Work could wait. He needed to be there for Nathan, now more than ever.

Worryingly, it soon became clear that there were other gaps in Nathan's memory, little glitches that caused the boy immense concern. It was very frustrating: one day he would recall something that had happened and the next he'd realise that he had forgotten something else. All Daniel could do was try to reassure him but he was worried to death that it wouldn't be enough. If the pressure became too great and Nathan went off the rails again…

It was Ellie who kept him grounded, only Ellie who could calm him and make him see beyond the bad bits so he could hope for the good. She never put any pressure on him by telling him that he shouldn't worry as everything would be fine: they both knew it wasn't true. However, she was always there, a calming presence in the background, and Daniel knew that he wouldn't have coped without her. He needed her so much, even though he felt guilty about taking what she offered when he had so little to give in return. At the end of the day, Nathan still came first.

Two weeks after the accident, Nathan was allowed home. Physically, he was perfectly fit, but mentally he was a different person. Daniel watched him like a hawk but there were no signs that he was going to relapse into his old ways and he grew quietly hopeful that they would get through it eventually. It was a big decision to return to work but Daniel knew that he had to do so if only to show Nathan that life could return to normal. Nathan was going into college that morning to talk to his tutors so at least he had the comfort of knowing where he was.

Marie greeted him with delight when he walked through the surgery doors. 'Hello, stranger! It's a wonder I still recognise you,' she declared, leaning over the desk to hug him.

'I know. It seems ages since I was last here,'

Daniel admitted, blanking out any thoughts about the nights he had spent at the flat above. The time he'd spent there was different, special. It had nothing to do with work.

'Good morning. It's good to have you back.'

His heart flip-flopped when he recognised Eleanor's voice. Although they hadn't managed to spend as much time together since Nathan had returned home, they had managed the odd occasion. Daniel was very conscious that Marie was watching them as he turned. Did Marie suspect that something was going on? he wondered, and then realised in surprise that he didn't care. What he and Eleanor had together had nothing to do with anyone else. It was their business, their pleasure. The thought unravelled the knot of tension inside him and he smiled.

'It's good to be back,' he said softly, his eyes meeting Eleanor's and holding them fast.

'That's nice to know.' Her smile was gentle and his heart managed to fit in another roll, like a seasoned circus tumbler warming up before a routine.

Just looking at her made him feel better, Daniel realised, made him feel more positive, more alive than he had felt for years, all the years since Camille had died. What did it mean? Was he in love with her?

Questions raced around his head, but it would take longer for the answers to come. It wasn't the questions that scared him after all, it was the answers, the fact he knew that once they came there could be no going back. He would have to make a decision then, make choices.

'Right. I'd better show willing and make a start. I'll see you both later.' Daniel made his way to his room and sat down at his desk, his thoughts in turmoil. How could he choose between Nathan and Eleanor? Yet that was what he would have to do. His heart felt like lead as he picked up the framed photograph that stood on his desk. It showed Camille and Nathan standing on a beach with their arms around each other, laughing. It had been taken during a family holiday to Cornwall, the last holiday they'd had together, in fact. Camille had been diagnosed with ovarian cancer

shortly after they had returned home and she had
been too ill to go on any more holidays.

Now Daniel felt his eyes fill with tears as he
looked at their smiling faces. He had honestly
thought their happiness would last for ever but
he'd been wrong. It had been snatched away from
them and there was no going back to those days.
Now he had a choice to make. He could put his
own happiness, the happiness he knew he would
find with Eleanor before everything else, including Nathan. Could he do it? Could he put himself first when it could have a detrimental effect
on his son?

'Oh, I'm sorry. I didn't mean to interrupt you
but I just wanted to make sure you saw the memo
I left for you.'

Daniel started when Eleanor opened the door.
There was no time to hide how emotional he was
feeling and he saw her eyes darken. Placing the
photo back on the desk, he stood up and went to
the sink, needing a moment to gather his thoughts.
'What memo was that?' he asked, making a great
production out of washing his hands.

'The one about Madeleine Walsh. A Dr Hamilton phoned while you were off. Apparently, Mrs Walsh has been referred to her privately for counselling. Dr Hamilton is convinced she is self-harming and she's worried because Mrs Walsh keeps missing her appointments. She wanted to know if you would mind having a word with Madeleine. Her phone number is on the memo if you want to call her back,' she added, starting to withdraw.

'I see. I'll phone her later.' Daniel made a determined effort to collect himself and dredged up a smile. 'It seems you were right about the situation, Eleanor, and I was wrong. I apologise for questioning your judgement.'

'It doesn't matter,' she said huskily. 'Being right isn't the be all and end all.'

She didn't say anything else before she left. Daniel frowned as he stared at the closed door. He had the feeling that there'd been more to that comment than first appeared. He sighed as he went and sat down again. What did it matter? He had more important things to worry about.

He had to make up his mind what he intended to do and he had to do it soon. It wasn't fair to Eleanor to leave her in this state of limbo.

CHAPTER FOURTEEN

SOMEHOW ELLIE MANAGED to get through the day, even though she wasn't sure how. Seeing the sadness on Daniel's face as he had studied that photograph had proved once and for all how stupid she was to hope that he would ever come to love her. Nobody could replace Camille in his life, and anyone who tried would only ever be second-best.

The thought made her feel sick. Several times she found herself almost overwhelmed by nausea but struggled to control it. However, by the time the day ended, her head was throbbing and she felt genuinely ill. Marie took one look at her and grimaced.

You don't look too good to me—are you OK?'

'I've got a headache, that's all.' Ellie drummed up a smile but it was a poor effort.

'You need some paracetamol or something,'

Marie declared. She looked over Ellie's shoulder. 'Ellie's got a headache, Daniel. Can you give her something for it?'

'Of course.'

Ellie didn't turn round. There was no need when she could hear the concern in his voice. Daniel might never love her but he cared about her and she knew he did too. Tears welled into her eyes because all of a sudden it was too much to bear. Daniel might care about her, but his heart still belonged to Camille and it always would. It was a moment of such utter despair that she couldn't contain her feelings and she saw the worry in his eyes as he bent over her.

'You should have said that you weren't feeling well!' He laid the back of his hand on her forehead. 'You feel rather hot to me. Do you have a temperature?'

'No. It's just a headache. I'm making a fuss over nothing. Sorry.'

The apology got swallowed up by a sob and the sob turned into another before she could stop it. When Marie rushed around the desk and led her to a chair, Ellie didn't protest. It was easier to let them think that she was ill rather than admit that her heart was aching, breaking, ripping itself apart. Daniel would never love her like he loved Camille. Deep down she had always known that but it hadn't stopped her falling in love with him, had it? The thought almost brought her to her knees. She had done what she had sworn she would never do and fallen in love with him!

'Here. Take these. They should take the edge off the pain.' Daniel's voice reflected his anxiety but Ellie knew that she mustn't make the mistake of reading more into it than that. She didn't say anything as she took the tablets, swallowing them down with some of the water that Marie fetched for her.

'It'll take about twenty minutes before they have any effect,' he said quietly. 'I'll help you upstairs so you can lie down and rest.'

'There's no need,' Ellie began, but he cut her off.

'Of course there is! It's all down to me that you're feeling this way, Eleanor—we both know that.'

Ellie flushed, hoping that Marie would attribute the comment to the extra work she had been doing during his absence. As far as she was aware, nobody knew about them and that was how she wanted it to remain. Licking her wounds in private when they parted would be preferable to doing so in public.

Marie fussed around, fetching her coat, finding her bag, and giving her advice. Ellie was touched when she offered to stay with her, even though she refused. She needed to be on her own to deal with this and it would make it all the harder if she had to pretend and hide how she was feeling. She had done that when she and Michael had split up. She hadn't wanted anyone to know how hurt she had been so she had played down her feelings. However, breaking up with Michael had been very different. Maybe her pride had been hurt but her heart had been intact. And it made it all the worse to realise it and understand that real heartbreak was a very different beast.

Ellie didn't say a word as Daniel led her out of the surgery and round to the flat. She had gone into this with her eyes open and it was her fault—

hers alone—that she had believed she could handle it when it ended. When Daniel asked her for the key, she handed it over, too heartsick to refuse. This was the end for them and she knew it was, knew it had to be because she couldn't carry on, not now she knew for a fact that he would never love her like he had loved his late wife. No, it was better to let him go now rather than wait until later and suffer even more.

'I wish I could stay.' Daniel opened the door, his face reflecting the battle he was having, concern for her warring with his need to take care of Nathan. 'But I have to get back to Nathan, Eleanor. I'm so sorry.'

'Of course you do.' Ellie nodded then winced when her head throbbed even harder.

'You do understand, don't you?' He touched her cheek, his fingers brushing her skin, so lightly, so gently, so familiarly that she could have wept all over again. She remembered every touch, every caress; they were as familiar to her as the feel of her own skin.

'Yes. You go, Daniel. I'll be fine. Really.'

'You're sure? Promise that you'll ring me if you feel any worse.'

'I'll be fine,' she repeated, desperately wanting him to go so that she could grieve in peace. 'You go and check on Nathan then I can stop worrying about how he is too.'

'I will.' He dropped a kiss on her mouth, taking her words at face value, thankfully. 'I'll see you tomorrow, although you're not to come in if you still feel rotten. OK?'

'Uh-huh.' Ellie managed to smile, even managed to hold it until he had gone down the steps, but once he disappeared that was it. Sobs tore at her throat as she closed the door, dry racking sobs that seemed to come from somewhere deep inside her. She stumbled into the bathroom and was violently sick then leant against the basin, shuddering and shaking as she wondered where she would find the strength to keep going, but what choice did she have? She had to learn to live without Daniel because he would never be hers.

Ellie made her way to the bedroom and lay down on the bed, too exhausted to undress. The painkillers were starting to work and the head-ache was easing enough to let her think. She had to work out what she intended to do. She couldn't stay in Beesdale—that was obvious. No, she would have to find another job, preferably abroad because that would be easier than remaining in England and allowing herself to carry on hoping. She and Daniel were over. What they'd had was finished. The sooner she accepted that, the better.

She drifted off to sleep only to wake in the middle of the night with her heart racing. Somewhere during those bleak hours a thought had surfaced: she had felt sick and nauseous all day. She had also missed a period. Was it possible that she was pregnant?

It turned out that Daniel's fears about how Nathan might have fared at college had been groundless. Far from unsettling him, it appeared that the chat with his tutors had reassured him. He was in a buoyant mood when Daniel got home and cheer-fully informed him that he intended to carry on with his studies and, if there were bits he had forgotten, well, he would just have to learn them again.

It was a huge relief, although Daniel knew it was too early to relax. Nathan could change his mind if he encountered a major setback so no way was everything cut and dried. However, it did help to relieve some of the tension he had been under for the past few weeks. Maybe the situation wasn't as dire as he'd thought it was. Maybe Nathan could cope with the idea of him having a relationship with another woman. After all, Nathan seemed to genuinely like Eleanor so perhaps it wouldn't be as stressful for him as Daniel had thought.

If he handled things slowly and gave Nathan time to come to terms with the idea, it could work. He desperately hoped so. Not only did he owe it to Eleanor not to string her along, he owed it to himself as well. It was about time that he enjoyed some personal happiness again. He went into work the following morning, feeling more upbeat than he had felt in a very long time. Marie was setting up for the day and she grimaced when she saw him coming in.

'Ellie just phoned to say that she still feels rotten so she's taking the day off. I offered to go up and make her some breakfast but she said she'd rather be on her own.' Marie lowered her voice when an early patient arrived for a fasting blood test. 'Apparently, she's got some sort of sickness and diarrhoea bug, the poor love.'

'Maybe I should pop up and check on her,' Daniel said in concern.

'I wouldn't. I got the impression that she'd prefer to be on her own. I can't say I blame her. I wouldn't want anyone watching me throwing up or worse!'

'All right,' Daniel conceded reluctantly, although he would have preferred to see for himself how Eleanor was. However, the last thing he wanted was to embarrass her.

He went to his room, aware that it wouldn't make any difference to how he felt to see her at her worst. He would wipe her brow, soothe her, care for her, and be happy to do so too. After Camille had died, the one abiding thought that had filled his mind was that he couldn't go through an experience like that again. But he could. And he would if Eleanor needed him. If that wasn't love, *true* love, then what the heck was it?

The thought settled into his mind, filled the gaps and the empty spaces not with fear, as he had expected, but with joy. He loved Eleanor. He loved her without reservations, without doubts or regrets. He and Camille had had their time and he would never forget it, always cherish it, but now it was time to look to the future. With Eleanor. If she would have him, please, God.

Ellie spent the day holed up in the flat. Although she genuinely felt sick, the rest was pure invention. She simply couldn't have gone into work and faced Daniel wondering if she was pregnant. She would have to buy a pregnancy testing kit and find out for definite, although she knew deep down it was true. The missing period, the sickness and nausea, the fact that her breasts felt heavy and swollen were all indications. Although she was on the Pill there had been a couple of occasions when she had taken it later than normal after she had spent the night at Daniel's house and it was that which had probably caused it to fail. Once she knew for certain that there was a baby on the way then she could make plans, although one thing was certain: she had no intention of getting rid of it. Although she doubted if Daniel would want this child, she wanted it. Desperately. Caring for their son or daughter would give her a purpose and make all the heartache worthwhile.

Ellie managed to slip out in the middle of the morning and drove to a supermarket on the outskirts of a neighbouring town where there was less chance of her being recognised. She bought a pregnancy testing kit and drove back. She took the kit into the bathroom and followed the instructions, unsurprised when two pink lines appeared in the tiny window. So she was pregnant and now she needed to formulate her plans so that when Daniel came to check on her this evening, she knew exactly what she intended to do.

The last thing she wanted was him becoming

suspicious. Even if he didn't want this baby, she knew that he would want to do the right thing—offer to support her, maybe even suggest marriage. It would be so very tempting to agree and take what he offered and not worry about what he never could. However, Ellie knew that it would be unbearable to live her life knowing that he hadn't really wanted her, that he had simply done his duty. Better to be alone for the rest of her days than be second-best. When the knock on the door came shortly after six p.m. she forced herself to her feet. This was something she *had* to do. For her sake. For Daniel's sake. And, most important of all, for the sake of their child. She didn't want their child to grow up feeling that it wasn't truly wanted.

'How do you feel?' Daniel asked as soon as she let him in.

'Not too good,' she told him because it was true. She felt as though she could drop down dead on the floor, although it wasn't some horrible bug that was making her feel this way but a broken heart.

'I wanted to come up and see you before, but Marie said you wanted to be on your own.'

'I did. Chucking up and racing to the loo is not a good look,' she replied offhandedly. 'Not even in front of friends.'

'I thought we were more than friends, Eleanor,' he said quietly, his brows drawing together.

'Did you?' She shrugged. 'That's nice of you but let's not get carried away. We're friends—oh, and colleagues, of course, Daniel, or that's what we are in my eyes anyway.'

'I see. So these past few weeks, they've been what exactly? An expression of our *friendship*?'

His voice echoed with hurt, with disappointment and so many other emotions that Ellie almost gave in and begged his forgiveness. How could she lessen what they'd had, diminish it this way? It had been the most wonderful time she had ever experienced, the most magical, the most meaningful, but she couldn't tell him that when it could have devastating consequences for all of them. Daniel had to love her. He had to want her.

He had to *need* her for it to mean anything. Anything less wasn't enough.

'Probably. Oh, I know things got rather intense but, if we're honest, it was circumstances that made it that way, don't you think?'

She carried on when he didn't say anything, needing to fill the void before temptation proved too much and she told him the truth—how much she loved him, how much she wanted him, that she was willing to accept whatever crumbs he could give her rather than lose him. Maybe it would work for a while but it wouldn't work for ever, wouldn't be enough to know that she didn't own his heart as he owned hers. 'Nathan's accident was the trigger. We would never have got together if it hadn't happened, would we? It's better if we accept that and move on.'

'So that's what you want to do, is it?' he said harshly. 'Move on?'

'I think so.' She stared back at him, the tears falling in her heart where he couldn't see them. 'It was fun while it lasted but all good things have to come to an end. If we go back to what we were before—colleagues—then it will be simpler.'

'And what if I can't go back? What if I don't want to?' He stepped forward, his eyes blazing, although Ellie wasn't sure if it was anger or pain she could see in them. Probably a bit of both, she decided sickly. Daniel had every right to be angry. He had every right to feel hurt by what she was saying. He had held her, loved her, made her his, and he had earned the right to have an opinion. She just couldn't afford to listen to what that opinion was in case she weakened.

'Then I'm sorry but you'll leave me no choice other than to leave.' She stood up straighter, needing to look and sound convincing. 'I have no intention of staying somewhere where I feel uncomfortable. I'd rather look for another job than find myself in that position.'

'In that case I suggest you start looking immediately. Don't worry about working out your contract. I shall be happy to release you.'

He wrenched open the door, his face set, his body rigid. That he was furiously angry was bad enough but that he was deeply wounded as well was more than she could bear. Ellie half reached towards him but he ignored her as he ran down the steps. Ellie closed the door, listening to the sound of a car engine being revved to within an inch of its life. Daniel was furious with her and no wonder. He probably felt betrayed, cheapened, insulted, the whole damned lot, but he couldn't feel any worse than she did. She bit her lip to hold back another desperate sob. *His* heart wasn't broken but *hers* was.

CHAPTER FIFTEEN

DANIEL COULDN'T BELIEVE what had happened. No matter how many hours he spent each night thinking about it, he couldn't believe it. Eleanor didn't love him. She didn't want him. She had no intention of spending her life with him!

It was work that kept him going, work and his need to carry on for Nathan's sake. However, he knew that he would reach a point where he would have to let go, give in and grieve. He just needed to stave off the moment because he didn't want anyone to witness his devastation and especially not Eleanor. He couldn't bear to think that she might imagine he was playing the sympathy card. He might not have much left but he did have his pride!

The atmosphere in the surgery grew so tense that he knew people were speculating about what had happened between him and Eleanor. That they had their own theories didn't concern him, although he did worry about the effect it could have on team morale. He did his best to put a positive spin on things but he felt too raw to be positive, too wounded to sound hopeful.

As for Eleanor, the best he could say was that she was reserved. She was unfailingly polite with everyone, him included, but she held herself at one step removed. There was no idle chit-chat, no gossip, just work. It made him long for the day she would tell him that she was leaving at the same time as he dreaded it. Could losing her physically really be any worse than her cutting him out of her life like this?

When the day arrived, it was pouring with rain. The River Bees had breached its banks and there was widespread flooding throughout the area. Daniel couldn't help thinking how fitting it was that she should have chosen this day to leave. Even the heavens were crying.

'I've found another post.' She came into his room without bothering to knock, proof of how eager she was to get this show on the road. 'A practice in Surrey is desperate for cover over Christmas and the New Year and I've agreed to do it.'

'I see. So you've decided to go for a short-term contract,' he said as calmly as he could, not that he cared how long the wretched contract lasted. She was leaving and that was all that mattered.

'Yes.' She shrugged as she pushed back her hair, which had grown longer since she had been at The Larches, and it suited her...

'Sorry. Say that again,' Daniel instructed as his mind drifted off. What did it matter how she looked? She didn't give a damn about him or his opinions, as she had made it abundantly clear.

'I've decided to apply for a job overseas eventually, Australia probably, although I haven't made the final decision yet so it could be New Zealand.' She met his eyes. 'It's something I've thought about before and now seems like a good time to do it.'

'If that's what you want,' he said neutrally, although the thought was making his heart race. If she went overseas he would never see her again and he wasn't sure if he could bear it.

'It is. Anyway, I'm leaving at the end of the week, if that's all right with you? I know it's short notice but you did say that you'd be willing to release me from my contract,' she reminded him briskly.

'I did and I shall.' Daniel stood up and offered her his hand because that was all he could offer her when she didn't want his heart. The thought made him feel all choked up but he hid it well. 'I wish you every success wherever you go, Eleanor. You've made a valuable contribution while you've been here and I appreciate it.'

'Thank you.' She started to leave, paused, half turned back, and then shrugged. 'Thank you too, Daniel. I've enjoyed working with you.'

Only enjoyed? he wanted to ask, but didn't because there was no point when it wouldn't change anything. He sat down after she left, feeling worse than he had felt in his entire life. He felt cold and empty and desperately alone. What made it all the worse was that he had allowed himself to hope, to dream, to *want* more than he would ever have. If he couldn't have Eleanor, he didn't want anyone else and he never would.

Eleanor just made it back to her room before the tears came. She let them pour down her face, needing the release from all the tension. She had done what she'd had to do and now there was no turning back, no second chances, no reason to hope that there might be a better solution, one that wasn't so painful.

She would get through this for the sake of her child, a little boy or girl who needed her to be strong. She would love and care for it, make sure he or she knew that it was wanted, cherished. She understood how it felt to feel that you weren't enough and her baby would never be allowed to feel lacking in any way. She would give this child all the love it needed, love it to eternity and beyond, love it enough for her *and* Daniel. No child would be better loved. She would make sure of that!

It was Friday afternoon and the day Eleanor was leaving when Daniel decided to visit Madeleine

Walsh. It was a premeditated decision. If he visited Mrs Walsh, he could collect Nathan from college afterwards and then drive straight home. He wouldn't have to return to the surgery, wouldn't need to speak to Eleanor and wish her well before she left. He could get that over with at lunchtime and maybe it would help lessen the impact in some way.

He kept it brief, shook her hand, thanked her, and left. Marie was muttering something about them all meeting up for a drink that night but he pretended not to hear. He wasn't going to sit in the pub and celebrate, neither was he going to drown his sorrows with a pint of best bitter. He was going to handle Eleanor's departure with dignity even if it killed him!

He drove out of the surgery, taking the road to Hemsthwaite as the Walsh family lived that way. The rain was lashing down and the River Bees was overflowing, muddy brown water swirling over the banking and across the road. Potholes had formed where the tarmac had been washed away and Daniel slowed down as he tried to steer around them. He had almost reached the turning to Cherry Tree Lane when the road gave way, a huge chunk of it falling into the swirling river. Daniel had just seconds to react and he wasn't quick enough, probably because his mind wasn't focused when he was thinking about Eleanor and her imminent departure. He swerved to the right, praying the tyres would find something to grip onto, but more of the road collapsed. All of a sudden he felt himself floating, the car spinning round and round as though he was on some kind of crazy fairground ride, like those teacups that Nathan had loved as a child…

The car hit a tree and Daniel hit his head on the side window. Teacups and water and roads that were collapsing suddenly started to jumble themselves up together and he had no idea what was real any more. It was a relief when blankness descended on him and he could no longer see, think or feel. There was less pain that way, less heartache, maybe even a smidgeon of hope. Maybe there was a way to stop Eleanor leaving if it wasn't too late.

* * *

Eleanor was in her room, trying to come up with an excuse not to go to the pub that night, when Marie came rushing in to find her.

'There's been an accident!'

'An accident,' Ellie repeated blankly like some fifth-rate actor struggling to remember her lines.

'Yes! It's Daniel. The road's collapsed and his car's been swept into the river.'

It took a second, one precious second that Ellie knew she would relive over and over again, before she reacted. She shot to her feet, her heart racing in fear. 'Is he all right? They've got him out, haven't they?'

'Yes, but it was a close call. If Philip Applethwaite hadn't seen what happened... Well, it doesn't bear thinking about! Apparently, Phil and one of his lads—Steven, the youngest—waded in and managed to get a chain on the car while it was wedged up against a tree and they pulled it out with their tractor. A couple of seconds later, the tree disappeared.'

Ellie sank down onto the chair as her knees buckled. 'Where is he?' she whispered hoarsely.

'Daniel?' Marie gave her a funny look. 'They've rushed him off to Leeds. York's flooded and the ambulances are being diverted wherever they can squeeze them in.'

'I'll get straight over there.' Ellie stood up and gathered up her bag. She was halfway out of the door before Marie spoke.

'Wouldn't it be easier to phone and ask how he is?'

'I need to see him.'

'Ah. Right. I get the picture.' Marie smiled smugly. 'I *thought* something was going on. Seems I was right.'

Ellie had no idea what she meant and didn't wait around to ask. She had to get to the hospital and check that Daniel wasn't badly hurt. A sob caught in her throat but she didn't have time to cry when she needed to drive there. The journey seemed to pass in a trice, even though it took hours to ne-gotiate the flooded roads and all the traffic. She parked outside on the road, not caring if the car would be towed away. Daniel needed her. That was more important than anything else.

A and E was frantically busy but she persisted until she found a young nurse who knew where Daniel was. She followed her along the corridor, around the corner, and there he was, lying on a trolley, eyes closed, a huge dressing covering the right side of his head. Ellie didn't know if she felt relieved or what. He was obviously injured but he was alive and, so help her, he was going to stay that way. No way was she going to let him go now, not after this, after being so scared, so shocked, so utterly and completely devastated. Even if he could never love her the way she wanted, it would be enough. She would make sure it was!

She walked straight over to the trolley, bent down and kissed him on the mouth because this wasn't the time to play games. This called for the truth, every tiny, scary bit of it. 'How *dare* you do this to me, Daniel?' she said furiously when he opened his eyes and stared at her in surprise. 'How bloody *dare you* scare me to death like this?'

There was a moment when he didn't react and then he smiled. Slowly, wolfishly, smugly. 'I was right then. It was all an act. You love me, don't you, Eleanor?'

'Yes,' she hissed, unwilling to let him off the hook after she had suffered such torments, and his smile grew bigger, bolder, even more confident before it turned into a laugh.

'Then it seems we're quits,' he murmured, his eyes holding hers as he slid his hand round the back of her neck and drew her down to him. 'Because I, Eleanor Munroe, love you too, you bloody annoying woman!'

The nurse somehow managed to find them a space in cubicles. Daniel had a sneaking suspicion it was embarrassment at the sight of people their age making out that prompted her to redouble her efforts. Granted, any privacy was illusory with only paper curtains to separate them from the patients in the adjoining cubicles but Daniel could ignore them if he couldn't see them. After all, he only had eyes and ears, and everything else, for Eleanor.

He kissed her again, slowly and deeply to make up for the torment he had suffered these past terrible weeks. After they drew apart, he waited while she pulled up a chair then took hold of her hand. 'Why?'

'Because I was afraid.' She didn't ask him what he meant—she knew. And the pain released its grip that bit more because they were so in tune that they didn't need to explain the important bits.

'That I didn't love you?' he said simply, and felt her shudder.

'Yes. I knew when I saw you with that photo that you could never love me as much as you loved Camille.'

'That isn't true.' He squeezed her fingers, only slackening his grip when he felt her wince.

'Isn't it?' she said in a lacklustre voice that cut him to the quick.

'No. I'll admit that how I feel about you is very different from how I felt about Camille. I loved her and I would have carried on loving her if she hadn't died. But she did.'

'Then how can I ever measure up to her? I can't compete with her, Daniel. I wouldn't try!'

'Good, because this isn't a contest. This is something far more important than scoring points, for me as well as for you.' He lifted her hand and kissed her knuckles, one by one, then placed their joined hands on the side of the bed. 'Camille and I were very young when we met. I was twenty-two and she was nineteen. We fell in love and grew up together, loving one another.'

'It must have been a wonderful time,' she murmured, her voice catching.

'It was. There's something magical about first love, but it doesn't mean you can't fall in love again and that it won't be just as special, maybe even more so.'

'More so?'

'Yes.' He leant over and kissed her, ignoring the throbbing in his temple. What did a bit of pain matter when he needed to sort out the rest of his life? 'The moment I met you, Eleanor, I knew you were trouble. I felt all shaken up, tense, on edge.' He laughed at her stunned expression. 'I think I have some idea how Sleeping Beauty must have felt when she was woken by her prince—totally and utterly discombobulated!'

He carried on when she didn't reply, knowing how hard she must find it to believe what he was saying. A wave of tenderness swept over him and he smiled. Heaven knew, he understood how she felt. He'd had the devil of a job getting *his* head around it and he'd had weeks, whereas he had just landed this on her without any warning. 'The trouble was that I hadn't expected to feel this way—ever. I'd settled for what I saw as my lot in life—i.e. widower, father, doctor, et cetera. I wasn't looking for more—I didn't want more, to be honest. But then you came along and there was something about you that made me start wishing for things that I wasn't sure I could or even should have.'

'You felt guilty?' she said quietly. 'About letting go of Camille and seemingly forgetting her?

I would *never* expect you to do that, Daniel! I know how much she means to you and Nathan...'

'I know you do. That's why you're so special and why I can't bear to live the rest of my life without you.' He took a deep breath as all the emotions he'd held in check swirled to the surface. It felt as though they were choking him but he had to keep going, had to make sure that Eleanor understood how much he loved her.

'I fell in love with you, Eleanor, because I couldn't help myself. Yes, it scared me and, yes, I was stricken with guilt as well as fear about how Nathan would react if I had a relationship with you. But, despite all that, I couldn't not fall in love with you. You're the matching beat of my heart, you're the breath in my lungs, the heat in my blood. You're part of me and I can't live without that part because it's too hard. What I feel for you is warm and gentle and tender and sweet. It's also burning hot and all-consuming and it will continue to burn just as hotly even when we're old and grey, sitting side by side in matching bath chairs. There isn't a bit of you that I don't love, don't want, won't cherish. If you'll have me.'

Ellie could feel tears stinging her eyes even as a huge great wave of elation consumed her. Daniel loved her. He *really* loved her! She wasn't second-best but first choice, the woman he had chosen, the woman he would love for ever and always. Leaning over, she kissed him, letting her lips tell him how she felt, how overjoyed, how happy, how relieved. It was several minutes before she pulled away, although it could have been a lifetime too. It felt like it, felt as though she had been reborn as a whole new woman, the woman Daniel loved. She realised then that she had to tell him about the baby, that this was the perfect moment to layer joy on joy until it grew so huge that nothing could sweep it away. She and Daniel were going to have a child. He deserved to know just how wonderful their future was going to be!

'I've something to tell you,' she said quietly but without hesitation. 'I'm pregnant, Daniel. I'm carrying our child.'

'You...me...we...a *baby*!' The words came out

in a rush, shock rippling the edges, but it was no competition for all the other emotions she could hear as well. Then all of a sudden he was standing up, drawing her into his arms, holding her close, kissing her and talking at the same time. 'I had no idea… I never suspected… Is *that* why you were leaving?'

It was easier to answer the last question first. 'Yes. I thought it was unfair to drop it on you when you didn't love me.'

'Oh, Eleanor. Darling! I can't imagine what you've been through these past weeks.' He cupped her cheek, tears pouring down his face. 'Thank you. You were mad to do such a crazy thing but I understand why you did it.'

'Because I love you too much to hurt you or cause you any pain. I also couldn't bear to think that you'd do the right thing out of a sense of… well, duty,' she admitted, not wanting to make it appear that she had been thinking solely about him and not even a little bit about herself.

'Damn! Does that mean that I can't do the right thing now, even though it's the thing I want to do more than anything else? Talk about boxing me into a corner!'

Ellie was feeling a little lost. Maybe it was the rush of emotions, Daniel's confession, and everything else, but she was finding it difficult to follow what he was saying. 'I'm sorry but I'm not sure what you mean.'

'Then I need to make myself clear.' He smiled into her eyes and she felt her heart catch when she saw the love in his. 'I should by rights be down on my knee, ring in one hand, rose in the other, with violins playing in the background, but somehow I don't think that's going to happen, so here goes. Eleanor, my love, my darling, will you marry me?'

'Marry you?' she repeated blankly.

Yes. Oh, I know it's old-fashioned in this day to get married and that a lot of people live perfectly happily without doing so, but it's not what I want.' He drew her to him and kissed her tenderly. 'I want to make a proper commitment to you and our child. I want to spend the rest of my life loving you and caring for you and knowing that we shall always be together. I always wanted another child but it simply didn't happen so this is like a double blessing. To be loved by you and to have our baby as well is more than I could have dreamed of.'

'It's more than I could have dreamt of too,' Ellie whispered, almost too moved by the admission to speak.

'So does that mean you will marry me?'

'Yes!' The word shot out of her mouth as her voice came rushing back. When Daniel bent and kissed her again, it seemed to put the seal on her happiness. She was going to marry him and they would raise their baby together, loving and caring for each other. She had everything she had ever wanted and more!

EPILOGUE

'NOW, ARE YOU sure you've got everything? Passport, money, phone…?'

'Yes! I've also got a clean hanky and been to the loo and had a pee.' Nathan rolled his eyes. 'Chill out, Dad. I'm going to Australia, not the moon.'

Ellie chuckled. They were at Manchester Airport, waiting for Nathan to board his flight to Perth. He had decided to take a gap year before starting university. It was only a delay, he'd assured them. He had no intention of skipping out. But, as he had explained, he needed to find out who he was before he decided who he wanted to be.

Although most of the memory lapses had resolved themselves, there were a couple of incidents he couldn't recall and might never do so. However, he was philosophical about it and accepted that some areas might always be blank. The strange thing was that losing bits of his own memory had triggered an interest in helping others in a similar position and he was thinking about switching courses and working in that field. He'd had an interview at Liverpool and despite the fact that he would need an extra science subject, they had offered him a place studying medicine the following year. Ellie knew that he must have impressed them to have been given such an opportunity but, there again, he was turning into a very impressive young man, just like his father was.

She glanced at Daniel, feeling her heart lift as it always did whenever she looked at him. They had got married at the end of November, a simple ceremony held at Beesdale Parish Church. Her whole family had attended, even her sister. She and Gemma had had a long talk about past issues and, to Ellie's surprise, Gemma had admitted that she'd always felt jealous because their parents had *chosen* her, whereas she was just their natural child and nothing special. They had laughed about it and it had healed the rift that had existed between them since childhood. When Gemma had asked if she could be her bridesmaid, Ellie had readily agreed. Now that she was having a baby of her own, she wanted all her family around her.

'Right. Time to go. And, yes, I shall be in touch for an online video chat every single evening or I will unless I'm too busy enjoying myself to think about aged parents back home—not meaning you, obviously, Ellie,' Nathan added, winking at her.

'Obviously not,' she agreed dryly. That Nathan had accepted her relationship with Daniel and been thrilled when he had learned about the baby had doubly endeared him to her. She had no hesitation as she reached out and hugged him. 'Have a brilliant time. We're here if you need us, but I know you won't, so just enjoy yourself.'

'I will.' Nathan hugged her back, sounding ever so slightly choked. 'You've brought the fun back into my life as well as Dad's and I love you for it.' He let her go before things got too mushy, grinning broadly as he looked pointedly at her bump. 'Just make sure this little one doesn't play you up.

Kids can be a trial. I'm talking from experience here, so I know!'

'Oh, I'm sure we'll cope when your sister arrives,' Daniel declared airily, getting his own back. 'Girls aren't nearly as much trouble as boys.'

'It's a girl? When did you find out?' Nathan demanded, sounding for all the world like a ten-year-old who had missed out on a treat.

'When I went for my twenty-week scan,' Ellie admitted, laughing. 'Your dad insisted that we shouldn't tell you until today. A sort of farewell gift.'

'More like an attempt to get one over on me,' Nathan declared grumpily, then suddenly laughed. 'That is *so* cool! I'm going to be a big brother to my very own baby sister. I can't wait!'

'I'm afraid you're going to have to,' Daniel declared, stepping forward to hug him. 'But don't worry, it won't be long now and we'll keep you posted—make sure you receive lots of bump photos et cetera.'

'I think I can live without them—just!' Nathan hugged Daniel back. 'Thanks, Dad, for everything. I know I've been a real pain in the backside but you never gave up on me and I won't forget it.'

'It was what I wanted to do,' Daniel told him truthfully. 'I love you too, son, and nothing will ever be too much trouble where you're concerned. I just want you to be happy. That's all I ask.'

'I shall.' Nathan picked up his bag, kissed Ellie again, then went to join Jack and a couple of others who had decided to enjoy a year of freedom before knuckling down to work. They were laughing and joking as they headed off to security.

Daniel felt his eyes prickle with tears as he watched them leave but in his heart he knew that Nathan was going to be fine. Now it was time to think about Eleanor and their new little daughter. Happiness fizzed through his veins. A world that had once seemed grey and bleak now seemed to be filled with light and colour. Sliding his arm around Eleanor's shoulders, he drew her to him, kissed her, held her, and smiled as he said softly, 'Shall we go home?'

'What a good idea.'

She snuggled against him as they left the terminal. It was still very early and although there was traffic about there seemed to be an odd sense of peace hanging over the place. But maybe the peace came from within, Daniel mused, came from his heart, from his soul, from his love for this woman who had given him her heart and taken his in return.

He breathed in deeply, not tasting the vapours of aviation fuel or the emissions from countless car exhausts. All he could taste was happiness and it had a very special flavour, one he intended to enjoy over and over again. For ever.

* * * * *

If you enjoyed this story, check out these other great reads from Jennifer Taylor

REAWAKENED BY THE SURGEON'S TOUCH
THE GREEK DOCTOR'S SECRET SON
MIRACLE UNDER THE MISTLETOE
BEST FRIEND TO PERFECT BRIDE

All available now!